BILL & FRED?

John Quinn

THE O'BRIEN PRESS
DUBLIN

First published 2005 by The O'Brien Press Ltd,
20 Victoria Road, Dublin 6, Ireland.
Tel: +353 1 4923333; Fax: +353 1 4922777
E-mail: books@obrien.ie
Website: www.obrien.ie

ISBN: 0-86278-915-X

Text © copyright John Quinn 2005
Copyright for typesetting, layout, editing, design
© The O'Brien Press Ltd

British Library Cataloguing-in-Publication Data
Quinn, John, 1941-
Bill and Fred?
1.Sisters - Juvenile fiction 2.Snooker - Juvenile fiction
3.Children's stories I.Title
823.9'14[J]

1 2 3 4 5 6 7 8 9 10
05 06 07 08 09

The O'Brien Press receives
assistance from

the arts
council
schomhairle
ealaíon

Layout and design: The O'Brien Press Ltd
Printing: Cox & Wyman Ltd

CONTENTS

CHAPTER ONE

Invitations. They didn't look like invitations. They looked like pieces roughly cut from a roll of pale blue wallpaper – which is what they were. But they were invitations, too. A simple message was written on the back of each piece:

Bill and Fred
invite you to meet them
at Walburley Hall
this Saturday 3–5pm.
Come and meet
your new neighbours!
Refreshments served.

The 'invitations' had popped up all over the village in one day. They were in the post office where the

Lotto leaflets had been. They were in the church porch where the parish newsletters had been. They were in the supermarket where the entry forms for the soup competition had been. And in the chemist's shop in the box which said, '*At last – a cure for the common cold! Please take one.*'

Invitations. All over the village.

'What on earth is that?' Michael Lynch stared at the piece of blue paper propped up against the milk-jug on the breakfast table.

'Just what it says,' his wife Clare replied. 'An invitation to afternoon tea. Katie brought it home. She says they're all over the village.'

She interrupted herself to put her head around the kitchen door and call upstairs. 'Katie! Hurry up! Daddy's nearly ready to go!'

No answer.

'Katie! You'll be late for school!'

'I'm coming!' came the muffled reply.

'That child! I never know what she's doing up there.'

Michael Lynch was still staring at the blue paper. He swallowed a spoonful of cornflakes. 'But that's wallpaper. Blue wallpaper!'

'Don't speak with your mouth full, dear. Bad example for Gavin.'

The two-year-old in the high chair slapped his spoon into his cereal at the mention of his name.

'Gavin good boy!' he spluttered.

'Yes, Gavin's a good boy,' his mother agreed. 'And Daddy's a bad boy, giving bad example.'

She wiped the cereal from his bib.

'I mean, who *are* Bill and Fred? Didn't even give their full names,' Michael continued. 'And writing on wallpaper! What kind of old codgers are they?'

'I think it's cute,' Clare laughed. 'Full of mystery. Who said they were old, anyway? Maybe they're a pair of film stars or fashion designers?'

'Dream on! A pair of mean and miserable chancers, if you ask me. Anyway, I'll be on the golf course on Saturday afternoon, well away from Bill and Fred, whoever, or whatever, they are.'

❖   ❖   ❖

'Please, Mister Guppy,' Katie whispered. 'I really need your help today. It's Thursday. Maths and spelling test. Miss Reddy's favourite torture. And I forgot to learn my spellings.'

She coiled the tattered cloth snake gently into the hatbox.

'Yes, I know I forgot to learn them last week, too. Oh, please don't argue, Mister Guppy. Just help me. Make something happen. You can do it; I know you can. Now I have to go – Mummy's calling. I'm sorry I have to hide you away again, but you know why ...'

She put the lid on the hatbox and slid the box into the far corner of the wardrobe. She carefully stacked her books all around and over the box.

'Please, Mister Guppy. Make it happen,' she whispered as she settled her roller-skates on top of the book pile. 'You can do it!'

Her mother's voice called urgently from below.

'I'm coming,' Katie answered.

CHAPTER TWO

The car sped away through the misty morning, the windscreen wipers swishing back and forth, back and forth, clearing an arc of brightness through the drizzle.

'Bill and Fred! Bill and Fred!' Michael Lynch chanted to the rhythm of the wipers. 'An invitation to Walburley Hall – Wobbly Hall more like. Sure that old place must be in bits at this stage. Have you heard anything about this pair, Katie?'

'Which pair?'

'Which pair? Zig and Zag! Laurel and Hardy! Bill and Fred – the two old boys who are moving into Wobbly Hall!'

'No. I just found the invitation in the village.'

Her father gave a mocking laugh. 'Invitation! On wallpaper! Did you ever hear the like of it?' He put on a posh accent: 'Bill and Fred invite you to Wobbly Hall for further viewing of their wallpaper ...'

Kate wasn't listening any more. Her mind was on the maths and spelling tests. Every Thursday without fail Miss Reddy gave the tests: twenty maths questions and twenty spellings. 'We must make progress, children,' she would say. 'Progress, progress, progress. Who can spell progress for me? Katie?'

And then the results on Friday. More torture.

'We're not making progress, are we, Katie?'

Mister Guppy would *have* to make something happen. He would just have to.

Katie had had Mister Guppy for as long as she could remember. Aunt Joan had made him in her craft class from odd bits of material: yellow and brown and red and blue. Two big round green eyes and a yellow tongue were stitched on to his head.

'He's certainly a very colourful snake,' Katie's mother had said. 'Not that I like snakes very much.'

'He's not a snake,' Aunt Joan replied, slightly hurt at her sister's lack of enthusiasm for her handiwork. 'He's a draught excluder. And I'm quite proud of him!'

'A draught excluder?'

'Yes. You put him at the bottom of Katie's door to keep out draughts.'

'Oh, that's clever!' Katie's mother was impressed. 'I bet no one else in the whole village has something like that to keep out those nasty draughts – have they, Katie?'

Katie was very little at the time and didn't know what draughts were. She thought her mum and Aunt Joan were talking about giraffes. She knew about giraffes. They were very, very big and had really long necks. She had a picture of one in her Alphabet Book. G for Giraffe. How could giraffes come under your door? But if grown-ups said they could, then they could. And if grown-ups said they were nasty …

A bump on the road woke Katie from her day-dream. Her father was still going on about Bill and Fred.

'I didn't know there was anyone in Wobbly Hall. It's been empty for two – no, three years, since old what's-his-name died. Hardacre. Wasn't that his name? Hubert Henry Hardacre. Odd as a pot. The place was falling down about his ears for years and he wouldn't do anything about it. Wouldn't let anyone inside the door. Mad, he was. And now along come Bill and Fred No-Name! Must be as mad as old Hubert. *Bill and Fred No-Name, Wobbly Hall, Knockdown* – how's that for a name and address!'

CHAPTER THREE

The windscreen wipers swished even faster. Mister-Guppy. Mister-Guppy. Mister-Guppy. Katie drifted off again.

Why had she called him Mister Guppy? Something about a story her mother had read to her. There was a Mister Guppy in the story, but that was all she could remember. Whatever the reason, Mister Guppy was placed firmly against her door every night to keep those nasty giraffes out.

Once, when her parents had brought her to the zoo, Katie saw a real giraffe – from a distance. She wouldn't go anywhere near him. Her parents laughed.

'Oh, you are a silly,' her mother teased.

She wasn't a silly. Giraffes were nasty and would come in under your door at night if you didn't have a Mister Guppy to protect you. Mister Guppy was so brave. Katie told him so, every night.

And later, when she understood about draughts (she amazed Miss Reddy one day when she was the only one who could spell 'draught'. 'That's real progress, Katie. Well done!') and that giraffes didn't really come under your door, Mister Guppy was too good a friend to leave aside.

Now that he wasn't needed as a giraffe repellent, she took him into bed with her every night and told him about her day. She could really talk to Mister Guppy, and it seemed as though he actually listened to what she had to say. And if you really, really believed it, Mister Guppy could make things happen. Like when she wanted the new baby to be a boy – and along came Gavin. And when Katie didn't want Granny Lynch to go to heaven, she didn't. Not for a long while, anyway.

The trouble was, Mister Guppy grew worn and dirty. Several visits to the washing machine caused him to burst in places. Aunt Joan had got married and was living in France now, so Granny Lynch was given the job of sewing him up again. Eventually, Katie's mother lost patience with her.

'Really, Katie, you have the most expensive dolls and the nicest teddies and you still hang on to that *thing*. I never liked it from the day it came here. Aunt

Joan and her craft class! It's got to go. You're too old for it now, anyway. It's just ridiculous!'

The awful day came when Mister Guppy disappeared.

'I put him in the bin, where he belongs,' her mother said firmly. 'I told you–'

'No–o–o–o!' Katie screamed. She made straight for the rubbish bin.

'It's no use, Katie. He's gone. Today was bin-day.'

'I hate you! I hate you!' Katie shouted and ran to her room. She cried and cried for her lost friend until her mother could stand it no longer.

'Go away!' Katie yelled when she heard her mother at the bedroom door.

'Look, Katie,' her mother said. 'Look what I have.'

Katie lifted her tear-streaked face. Something dangled from her mother's outstretched hand. Something tattered – Mister Guppy!

'I told a little fib,' Clare Lynch admitted. 'I didn't actually put him in the bin.'

Katie swept him into her arms.

'But,' her mother continued. 'I am giving him back on one condition: I don't want to have to look at that creature any more, so please keep him out of my sight!'

And that was how Mister Guppy came to spend his days in the camouflaged hatbox at the back of the wardrobe.

❖   ❖   ❖

'We're here, dreamer!' Her father's voice roused Katie once more. 'Off you go!' He leaned over to give her a kiss. 'And remember – it's Thursday. Are you *Reddy* for your tests?' he chuckled.

'Yes, Dad.'

Every Thursday, the same joke.

'Bye!' Katie slung her bag over one shoulder and plodded up the path through the drizzle, ignoring Mr Carey's urgent ringing of the bell. She was last into her classroom.

Mr Carey, the school principal, followed immediately behind her. There was a loud hubbub in the room. Where was Miss Reddy?

'Right. Quiet, please. QUIET!' Mr Carey barked. 'Miss Reddy is, unfortunately, out sick today, so we'll divide you up. This row to Room One. This row to Room Two and this row to Room Four. Quickly and quietly, please.'

Katie couldn't believe it. She bounced along to

Room One. Wonderful, brilliant Mister Guppy had done it again.

'Thank you!' she whispered.

She knew that, in the darkness of the wardrobe, in the hatbox behind the books, he would hear her.

CHAPTER FOUR

'Ouch!' Shauna Lacy clutched her knee. This was the third time she had collided with the edge of the low table in the infants' classroom. And the small chair gripped her thighs so tightly that she wondered how she was ever going to get out of it again. Why did they have to be sent to Room One? Baby chairs. Baby tables. Twenty baby faces gave Shauna puzzled looks.

'These chairs are torture,' she whispered to Katie.

'Is something the matter down there?' the teacher called out.

'The chairs, Miss. They're too small for us. Can we get our own chairs from Room Three?'

'No. Too much clutter. You'll just have to make do. It's not that long since you fitted into those chairs.'

'Grrr,' Shauna muttered. 'Not fair.'

Katie smiled. She could put up with torture like this

as long as there were no tests. That was *real* torture.

Shauna had another idea. She raised her hand.

'Miss, can we go to the library?' she called loudly.

Twenty little faces turned to stare at her again.

'To get books—'

'Not now.' The teacher's patience was growing thin. 'Maybe at the break. Meanwhile, you can join in with the children in song-time.'

'This is soppy,' Shauna grumbled as she pretended to copy the infants who were happily shouting out the animal sounds in 'Old McDonald'.

'*With a moo-moo here and a moo-moo there—*'

'Imagine! A whole day of this!'

'Shush,' Katie said. 'It's fun!'

'*Eee-eye-eee-eye-o!*'

The teacher flipped over another animal picture. The children sang, '*And on this farm he had a donkey—*'

'Oh my God!' Katie shrieked. The startled faces turned around once more.

'What is it now?' the teacher snapped.

'Sorry, Miss, sorry,' Katie stuttered. 'I—I just remembered something. Sorry!'

'Any more interruptions and you two ladies will go straight to Mr Carey's room! Is that clear?'

'Yes, Miss. Sorry, Miss.'

The teacher flipped the picture chart back and started again.

Snowball! Katie had completely forgotten about Snowball. Her donkey. Well, the family donkey. Her father had won him in the 'Giant Parish Raffle'. He hadn't been too pleased with his prize.

'Typical!' her father had sighed. 'I spend twenty-five euro on tickets. I could win a weekend in a luxury hotel. I could win twenty golf lessons; a ton of coal, even. But no! What do I win? The most stupid prize of all. A stupid, stupid donkey!'

'*With a hee-haw here and a hee-haw there – everywhere a hee-haw,*' the twenty little voices chanted.

Snowball wasn't a stupid donkey. He was a very clever, kind and loveable donkey. He loved having people call to see him in his paddock. Katie visited him regularly. She usually brought him a treat – a carrot, a sweet apple – whatever she could smuggle from the kitchen. The trouble was—

'*With an oink, oink here and an oink, oink there,*' the din was growing louder.

—the trouble was that Snowball's paddock belonged to Walburley Hall. Nobody had lived there for the past few years, so there was no one to object to Snowball using the paddock. But now Bill and Fred were taking over. Suppose they didn't like donkeys? Suppose they had their own animals? Where was Snowball to go? Katie had been so worried about silly old tests that she had forgotten all about Snowball.

'*My bottom is KILLING me*,' Shauna sang as the infants roared out the last verse of 'Old McDonald'.

❖   ❖   ❖

'Did you have a nice day at school?' Katie's mother asked as they drove home.

'Miss Reddy wasn't in. We spent the day with the little kids, singing and playing and colouring.'

'Isn't that lovely?' her mother laughed.

'B-boring!' Katie said. She had been about to say 'better than spelling', but then she would have had to admit that she had forgotten to learn her spellings, again.

'Bo-ing! Bo-ing!' Gavin echoed from his baby seat.

'Can we go round by Snowball's paddock, Mum?'

'Oh, Katie, I have a million things to do.'

'Please? Just for a teensy minute?'

'See So-ball!' Gavin chanted excitedly. Gavin loved Snowball.

'Now look what you've started!' her mother sighed.

'All right. Just for one teensy minute.'

Snowball came to the paddock gate as soon as the car pulled up. His coat was wet and matted after the day's rain.

'Silly Snowball,' Katie said as she swept the water off his back. 'Why didn't you stay in your nice dry shed?'

The donkey nuzzled into her anorak in expectation of a treat.

'Sorry, Snowball. I didn't think I'd be coming today.' She lowered her voice to a whisper. 'I just wanted to tell you there are new people moving into the house. But don't worry. I'm sure they'll be very nice. Bill and Fred. They probably like donkeys a lot. Hope so, anyway.'

Her mother let down the back window and Katie urged Snowball forward so that Gavin could pat him on the nose. The donkey blew into the small boy's hand and Gavin chortled in delight.

'Teensy minute's up!' their mother announced.

'Bye, Snowball. Don't worry,' Katie called as she clambered into the car.

'I just remembered,' her mother said. 'You'll see Snowball on Saturday when we call to meet Bill and Fred. You didn't really need to see him today at all.'

Katie said nothing. She peered through the misty window beyond the trees where she could just make out the chimneys of Walburley Hall.

They had *better* like donkeys, she thought.

CHAPTER FIVE

Michael Lynch was in a foul humour. From early on Saturday morning the rain had poured down without stopping. There would be no golf today. Instead, he found himself driving his family to meet the new occupants of Walburley Hall.

'Isn't this fun?' his wife chirped. 'All of us going to meet our new neighbours.'

'Yeah, fantastic,' Michael Lynch growled. 'Going to meet two potty old fellows in a tumbledown house.'

'Oh, don't be such a stick-in-the-mud, Michael. It will be fun. And we'll get you a nice cup of tea for your headache!'

He knew by the way she said it that she didn't believe his story about the headache. He had hoped at least to get to watch the golf on television, but the excuse hadn't worked. He was sure he *would* have a headache before the afternoon had passed.

They turned into the long laneway that led to Walburley Hall. Katie strained to see Snowball through the rain-washed window. There he was. She could just make out his head poking out of the shed.

'Good fellow,' she whispered and she waved in his direction as they passed. Surely they would like him – who wouldn't?

❖   ❖   ❖

Walburley Hall looked grey and grim, made greyer and grimmer by the sheeting rain. Each window was shuttered, which gave the house a ghostly appearance. If it weren't for the line of cars parked along the front of the house, anyone would have thought that the building was empty and desolate, as it had been for the previous three years.

'At least we're not the only fools here,' Michael Lynch muttered, reversing the car onto the grass verge.

'They're probably all disappointed golfers, dear,' his wife replied, releasing Gavin from his car seat.

Katie led the way to the front door, dodging through puddles and skipping up the steps. A sign hung from the doorbell.

NOT WORKING – PLEASE KNOCK HARD!

She reached up to the knocker – a snarling lion's head – and slammed it down sharply.

'Katie! You'll wreck the door,' her mother protested.

'But it says "Knock Hard"'

The great door creaked open.

A very tall woman stood before them, dressed in trousers and a heavy woollen jumper. Her tanned face looked severe until it melted into a welcoming smile.

'Hello! Aren't you wonderful to come on such a dreadful day? Come in! Come in!'

The Lynch family gratefully stepped in from the rain.

'You can leave your wet things – umbrellas and stuff – here in the vestibule. And you are?'

'The Lynches. I'm Clare. This is my husband Michael. That's Katie and this –' she propped her son on her left arm '– is Gavin.'

'Gavin good boy!' he sang.

'I'm sure you are,' the tall woman laughed. There was a brief silence as raincoats and umbrellas were hung on the few remaining hooks.

'And you must be?'

'Oh, goodness me! How awfully rude of me! I'm Bill and – excuse me for a second!' She put her head around the door into the inner hall from where a hubbub of voices poured out.

Clare Lynch had to stifle a giggle, especially when she saw the look on her husband's face. Katie felt embarrassed.

'Mum, really!' she whispered.

'Yes. I'm Bill, and this is Fred!'

The tall woman led a smaller, plump woman into the vestibule.

'Fred, meet the Lynch family: Clare, Michael, Katie and Gavin, who is a good boy!'

'Gavin good boy!' he parroted.

The plump woman nodded nervously to the visitors and then looked anxiously at her sister.

'All right, Fred. Off you go and look after the guests!' The other woman hurried back into the hall.

'Fred's a bit of a worrier; always fretting that something awful might happen. Now, what can I get you? Tea, coffee, orange, lemonade? Some biscuits for a good boy?'

Clare Lynch tried hard not to look at her husband's face.

'A cup of tea would be lovely,' she said.

'Coffee, please. Strong, black,' Michael Lynch grunted.

'I'll have some orange, please,' Katie said, feeling she should apologise for her parents' behaviour.

'Lemolade! Lemolade!' Gavin cried.

'You shall have "lemolade", because you're a good boy,' the tall woman agreed. 'Come and join your friends!' She led the way into a large hall where the neighbours had gathered.

Michael Lynch rolled his eyes upwards and gave a despairing shrug of his shoulders.

'Dad, really!' Katie muttered. Parents – they always let you down.

❖   ❖   ❖

There was quite a gathering in the great hall. Clare and Michael nodded to familiar faces as they followed Bill in the direction of the staircase.

'Bill and Fred!' Michael Lynch muttered in disbelief. 'Bill and Fred! They're not two potty old fellows at all; they're two even pottier old women! Honestly! I've seen it all now!'

'Shush, dear. You'll be heard,' his wife whispered.

'So what? Isn't that what everyone's thinking?'

'Well not me, for one! I think they're rather cute. And what's wrong with being called Bill and Fred, anyway?'

'Because – because – oh, what's the use? Trust you to stand up for them.'

'Mum, Dad! Shush, please,' Katie pleaded. 'This is so–'

Katie was interrupted by Gavin tugging at her arm.

'Teddy! Teddy! Go see Teddy!'

'What teddy, Gavin?' This is so embarrassing, Katie thought. I want to be out of here.

'Big Teddy!' Gavin tugged harder and Katie stumbled after him.

He was right. Over beside the huge fireplace stood an enormous stuffed bear, so tall that he dwarfed every person in the hall.

'Hello, Teddy!' Gavin said, 'Nice Teddy! Big Ted!' He poked at the bear's furry legs.

The adults nearby watched in amusement.

Katie groaned inwardly. Can things get any worse? she wondered.

'Don't go for the orange drink!' a familiar voice whispered behind her. It was Shauna Lacy. 'It's only coloured water.'

'Am I glad to see you!' Katie sighed. 'But it's too late.

I've already ordered it.'

'And there's something else,' Shauna continued. 'You'll never guess—'

Gavin dragged impatiently at his sister.

'Kiss Teddy! Kiss Big Ted!'

'You can't, Gavin. I can't reach that far. Big Ted's too tall.'

Gavin's lower lip trembled. Katie knew that tears would follow. To her relief, she saw her father's arm beckoning her. Bill had arrived with a tray of drinks.

'Look, Gavin! Lemonade! Daddy's got lemonade for you.'

The pout became a smile. 'Lemolade for Teddy!'

Bill held the tray forward. 'Now, one tea, one coffee, one orange and one lemonade for the big man.' She beamed at Gavin. 'And a plate of biscuits.'

They took their drinks and Clare emptied Gavin's lemonade into the lidded plastic cup she had brought from home. She rescued the plate of biscuits before Gavin managed to grab them all.

Katie sipped her orange. Shauna was right. Coloured water.

'That will be three euro,' Bill added nervously.

Michael Lynch was, unfortunately, in the middle of a gulp of coffee. He spewed it back in a spray that rained down on Katie and Gavin.

'Dad!' Katie cried in disgust.

'You're joking!' Michael Lynch could barely utter the words.

'Not really,' Bill said, not meeting his eye. 'Fifty cent each for the drinks and a euro for the biscuits. That's three euro.'

'But, but that's daylight rob–'

'I'll hold your cup, dear,' his wife interrupted. 'I'm sure you have it in small change.' She did her best to stifle a smile.

'But–'

'If you haven't, I'm sure they have change.'

Michael Lynch rooted in his pocket and withdrew a handful of change. He still looked as though he expected a hidden camera to come out of somewhere. Surely this was a joke?

'There! I told you!' His wife handed him back his cup, picked out three euro coins and put them on Bill's tray.

'Thank you indeed,' Bill whispered and quickly melted away through the crowd.

'More biccies! Want more biccies!' Gavin cried.

Clare Lynch could no longer hold back her laughter.

'I don't know what's so funny,' her husband snapped.

'You are! It was the look on your face! I'll never forget it.' His wife had difficulty holding her cup steady.

'It's no laughing matter as far as I'm concerned. The cheek of them! Inviting people here and then charging!' He slammed his cup down on a nearby table.

'We're going home!' he announced. 'I didn't come here to be insulted.'

'Dad! Keep your voice down!' Katie pleaded. She was still mopping up the coffee spray.

'Oh, Michael, just see the funny side,' his wife laughed.

'We – are – going – home,' he repeated through gritted teeth as he began to move through the crowd towards the door. Clare Lynch sighed. There was no arguing with him in this mood.

'More lemolade!' Gavin held up his empty cup.

Their progress was halted by a loud handclap.

'Ladies and gentlemen, please!' Bill's voice rang out. She had ascended halfway up the staircase and held her hands aloft in a call for silence.

'If I could just have your attention for a few moments.'

The chatter subsided.

'Wait, Michael!' Clare Lynch tugged at her husband's sleeve. 'Let's hear what she has to say.'

'Probably charging us to get out,' he muttered.

'Be quiet, Dad!' Katie whispered. 'Someone will hear you.'

CHAPTER SIX

When the chatter finally faded away, there was a long pause before Bill began to speak.

'I – we – that's Fred and I – are not sure what to say, exactly. I think we should first of all apologise, as we seem to have offended some of you by charging money for the drinks.'

She paused again. The silence was broken by a PLINK-PLINK sound coming from the landing behind Bill. A large saucepan had been placed at the top of the stairs to catch a drip from the leaking roof overhead.

'Perhaps I should start at the beginning,' Bill continued. 'By telling you who we are and how we come to be here. Fred and I have spent all our lives in East Africa. We lived on a farm there, four of us – Father, Mother and us two. We did have an older brother but he died when he was six. It broke our father's heart. He looked on us as boys from then on. Called us Bill and Fred. We're really Wilhelmina and Frederika – our mother was Swedish – but we've been Bill and Fred for so long that we've forgotten how strange it sounds to people who don't know us ...'

PLINK! PLINK-PLANK! PLINK!

'Unfortunately, poor Father was more successful at drinking than farming, and by the time he died there was very little left. Then we had to nurse Mother for many years ... I'm sure you're finding this all very boring? Well, anyway, about a year ago, we heard that we had inherited this place. We knew nothing about Ireland or Uncle Hubert who owned Walburley Hall. It appears he was a cousin of Father's. We decided to leave Africa and come to live in Ireland. It took a lot of time and money to make all the arrangements. We have a little money left, but it seems there has been a delay in transferring it to Ireland. When we arrived and saw the condition of the place, we panicked a bit and came up with this idea of raising money and at the same time meeting you. We remembered our parents doing something like this when a neighbour's house was burned down. We realise now that it was wrong to do it here – but we did want to meet you all. We really did. So now, on your way out, you can reclaim your money from Fred. And thank you all for coming!'

There was an awkward silence.

PLINK! PLINK! PLINK!

A shuffling of feet towards the door was interrupted by a voice that startled Katie. It was her mother's voice.

'Wait! Wait a minute, please!'

Oh no, Katie thought. Not more embarrassment.

'I don't know if I speak for everyone,' her mother began, 'but I came here out of curiosity. I wanted to meet our new neighbours. I expected to meet two friendly old gentlemen – though I *secretly* hoped they were two thirty-something hunks!'

A titter of laughter ran through the crowd. Michael Lynch somehow forced a smile onto his face. Katie covered hers with her hand. Please, Mum. Enough!

'But what did I find?' Clare Lynch continued. 'Two absolutely charming women who I know will be happy here in Knockdown. I think they are very brave and very clever. What did they do wrong? Nothing. Nobody was held up and robbed. I've been charged more in Pat Mac's pub for a cup of coffee that was a lot colder!'

More laughter. Katie dared a look at her father. He

was squirming uneasily, looking this way and that.

PLINK! PLINK-PLONK!

'And my children enjoyed the biscuits! So what's the problem? None! You've done nothing to be ashamed of, Bill and Fred. We've had a nice time on a rotten afternoon. I say thank you, Bill and Fred. And welcome to Knockdown! We hope you'll be very happy here.'

There was a brief pause, then a ripple of applause. The ripple grew into a wave which echoed around the hall.

Katie found herself clapping loudly.

'Well done, Mum,' she called out. Sometimes parents are cool. Sometimes.

When the applause died down, faces turned towards Bill.

'Thank you. Thank you indeed.' Her voice was a little shaky. 'You are all very kind. I know Fred and I will like it here.' PLINK! PLONK-PLINK! 'There's still lots of tea and coffee – at no extra charge, but I'm afraid we're all out of biscuits.'

'Go see Big Ted!' Gavin cried as he tugged Katie's sleeve. The party was only beginning.

An hour later, the Lynch family said goodbye to Bill and Fred and made their way home.

'You were really cool, Mum,' Katie said, 'Making that speech.'

'Don't remind me,' her mother replied. 'I don't know what came over me. I never made a speech before in my life.'

'Well, it sure worked. Everybody had a good time and nobody looked for their money back. And Bill and Fred were very nice about Snowball too. They don't mind him being in the paddock. I can still come to see him whenever I like. So everything is cool.'

'Yeah, too cool!' Michael Lynch growled as he peered through the rain. 'How am I ever going to show my face in Pat Mac's pub again, after you made him the laughing stock of the village?'

'Nonsense,' his wife laughed. 'I'll bet you his coffee will be a lot warmer from now on!'

Katie squinted through the mist as they passed the paddock. Snowball turned his head to follow the car. You can stay, Snowball, she told him silently. Hurray!

Katie had been right about nobody looking for their money back. When Bill and Fred said goodbye to their last visitor, Fred retrieved the biscuit-tin money-box from the chair just inside the hall door. She was surprised at its weight.

'There's something wrong, Bill,' she said anxiously as she inspected the contents of the tin.

'What do you mean, "wrong"?'

'There seems to be much more money here than when I left it at the door.'

'Couldn't be. Let me see!' Bill poked through a mass of euro coins and found tightly rolled five- and ten-euro notes peeping out through the mound of silver. 'Goodness me! Goodness me!' she sighed. 'This is most embarrassing.'

'They obviously kept paying for the tea and coffee,' Fred said, 'and didn't even look for change!'

'Most embarrassing,' Bill repeated.

The surprises didn't end there. Over the next week, a variety of 'presents' appeared mysteriously on the steps of Walburley Hall. A sack of potatoes, bales of peat briquettes, a hamper of fresh vegetables, a box of tinned foods, two bags of coal … no names, no notes attached.

'Oh dear! This is all too much,' Bill exclaimed as she

opened the door to another present: a box of household cleaning materials, washing-up liquid, washing powder, polishes, sprays, soaps.

'It's only March but it feels like Christmas every day!'

❖   ❖   ❖

As Bill and Fred gradually opened more of the rooms in their new home and put to good use all the cleaning material their neighbours had supplied, the reasons why the local called it 'Wobbly Hall' became all too clear: squeaking, saggy floors, rattling windows, threadbare carpets, peeling wallpaper and doors that would not close. There was even a door that would not open: the key to the library had seized up in the lock.

'Don't sit in that sofa!' Bill called out as Fred plonked herself down after a tiring day's cleaning. Too late.

'*Yeeow!*' Fred jumped up in pain.

'Springs are gone,' Bill said quietly, 'but you know that now!'

After much oiling and coaxing by Fred, the key to the library finally turned.

'Well done,' Bill said as she stepped into the murky

room. She threw back the shutters and pulled aside the torn velvet curtains. Light flooded the room and revealed shelf after shelf of empty space where books should have been. 'Well, Uncle Hubert was no reader,' Bill concluded sadly.

There was something else down in the far corner of the room, covered by an old sheet. Even before she pulled the cloth back, Bill had guessed what that shape was, and her heart sank. She retreated quickly to where Fred was cleaning her oily hands.

'You don't want to go in there,' Bill said.

'More broken springs?' Fred enquired nervously.

Bill shook her head.

'Not another leak? We have no more saucepans.'

'No. Worse than that.'

Fred began to tremble. 'Not a body? A skeleton?'

Bill gave a hollow laugh.

'I wish it was! Oh, go on. See it if you must.'

Fred advanced cautiously. At first she didn't see it. Then her eyes slowly focused on Bill's discovery. She gave a yelp of joy.

'It can't be!'

'Unfortunately it is, and in surprisingly good condition, too.'

'It' was a full-size snooker table.

'Ohh! Ohh! Ohh!' Fred drooled.

'For goodness sake, Fred. Pull yourself together!'

'It's just so beautiful!' Fred stroked the green baize. 'Oh Bill, we haven't played since – since ...' her voice broke and trailed away.

I know all too well, Bill thought. Since we had to sell our table and everything else of any value to help pay off Father's debts. Father had taught them both how to play snooker at an early age. Trouble was, Fred always beat her sister at the game. Always. Always. Bill didn't like that. While she had been saddened to lose the table as part of their home, she was secretly delighted that she would never again be shamed by Fred's snooker skills.

Not until now.

'Oh look, Bill,' Fred cried with delight. 'The cues and balls are all here. May we have a game, please?'

'Now?'

'Yes, now. It's been so long. Please?'

'Here we go again,' Bill muttered and sank back into an armchair. *'Aaaagh!'* Unfortunately, another one with a broken spring.

CHAPTER SEVEN

'Voom! Voom!' Gavin was racing his cars along the windowsill. ' Voom—' suddenly he was distracted by two figures who were approaching the front door.

'Big Ted Mama! Big Ted Mama!' he announced excitedly to his mother in the kitchen.

'What on earth are you on about, Gavin?' his mother asked.

'Big Ted Mama!' As he spoke, the doorbell rang.

Katie heard Gavin from her bedroom. She immediately guessed what he meant and hurried downstairs.

'Big Ted's Mama indeed!' his mother said as she opened the door. 'Oh, it's—'

'Bill and Fred!' the tall woman on the doorstep said with a smile. 'We thought it was time we paid you a visit.'

'To thank you!' the smaller woman added.

'Well, come in, first of all!' Clare Lynch said as she gathered Gavin into her arms.

'Big Ted Mama!' he whispered in his mother's ear.

'You remember Gavin and Katie? Come in and make yourself at home. '

'We won't be staying long,' Bill said. 'As Fred said, we mainly want to thank you for your kind words at our welcome party.'

'It was nothing! I only said what people were thinking.'

'I doubt that,' Bill said with a laugh, 'but at least it made things happen!' She went on to explain about the mystery gifts that had been left at their door.

'What? That's wonderful!' Clare Lynch was delighted with the news.

'Wonderful, but embarrassing!' Bill said. 'But we are very grateful.'

There was a brief silence before Bill moved to go. Fred grasped her sister's arm and whispered in her ear.

'How silly of me! I almost forgot.' Bill spoke nervously now. 'It's about the donkey – your donkey!'

Oh no! Katie thought. They're going to put Snowball out of the paddock..

'Snowball?' Clare Lynch asked. 'Is he–?'

'He's fine. It's just that we found a little cart in one

of the outhouses and we wondered if we could use Snowball to get around, in return for the grazing in the paddock. You see, we have no car yet so it would be wonderful for us.'

'That's a great idea,' Clare Lynch replied. 'And of course it's fine with us. Isn't it, Katie? That donkey could do with a bit of exercise!'

'Sure!' Katie felt relief run through her body, although she wondered how Snowball was going to manage the load.

It was as if Bill read her mind. 'Don't worry. We're not that heavy!' She threw a playful look at her sister. 'And the cart is quite light. Now we really must dash. There's so much to do. Do you know there are out-houses we haven't been into yet? It's like a great big adventure.'

'My soup,' Fred said anxiously.

'Dear Fred,' her sister sighed. 'She put on a big pot of nettle soup before we left and is anxious to get back to it.'

'*Nettle* soup?' Katie blurted the words out without thinking.

'Of course! Bill makes the most wonderful nettle soup. And, believe me, we've got lots of nettles! Next time you visit, we'll have nettle soup especially for you.'

'That would be lovely,' Clare Lynch said, a little hesitantly. 'Now, may I offer you a lift home?'

'Not at all. Fred and I are used to walking. It's only a little way. In Africa, we walked miles and miles.'

Katie got the feeling that Fred might have been easily persuaded to take a lift. She felt Gavin tugging at her sleeve and bent down to hear his whisper.

'Go see Big Ted! Want Big Ted!'

'No, you can't, Gavin!' she whispered in reply. Gavin began to whimper.

'What on earth is the matter with you two?' their mother snapped.

'It's Gavin, he wants to see Big Ted again,' Katie explained.

'Who is this Big Ted?' Bill asked. 'He keeps going on about Big Ted.'

'It's your bear – the stuffed bear in Walburley Hall,' Katie explained.

Bill gave a hearty laugh.

'Big Ted! What a perfect name for him. Do you know, Uncle Hubert left a strict provision in his will that the bear was not to be moved from the Hall under any circumstances. In fact, it was phrased in such a way that it sounded like a warning. Let me think … there was a little verse …

Move not the bear from Walburley Hall,
Or else a tragedy will befall.

Yes, that's it. Doesn't make any sense, does it? Maybe poor old Uncle Hubert was as batty as everyone says he was. That old bear is only food for moths. He's bald in spots, and when you get close to him he's downright smelly! If I had my way he would be thrown out, but Fred here won't agree.'

'Uncle Hubert must have had a reason,' Fred argued. 'And we don't want a tragedy, do we?'

'Tragedy! Hmph!' her sister sniffed. 'You worry too much about *everything*, Fred. The only tragedy is that that bear has been there for far too long.'

She bent down to Gavin, who was now hiding shyly behind his mother.

'Of course you may come to see Big Ted, little man. Why don't you all come next Saturday and we'll have some of Fred's nettle soup?'

'That would be very nice,' Clare Lynch replied. 'Wouldn't it, children?'

As she watched Bill and Fred stride up the road, Katie could only think of her mouth and tongue being stung by nettles as she tried to tell Fred how delicious her nettle soup was. Nettle soup! *Yeuck!*

❖　　❖　　❖

During the course of the following week, the people of Knockdown grew accustomed to the unusual sight of the two ladies arriving in the village on a donkey and cart.

They would park Snowball outside the post office or the grocer's and do whatever business they had to do before trotting off home again. People were inclined to mock at first, particularly the regular inhabitants of Pat Mac's pub, who had a smart remark ready for every occasion.

'I wonder if they're taxed and insured!'

'What do you think of the sunroof, lads?'

'I'd say it's a '99 model – an 1899 model!'

'I might ask them for a lift home – but I'd be quicker walking!'

But most of the villagers were soon won over by the sisters' pleasant manner.

'Sure, they're a bit unusual, but there's no harm in them.'

'Well, fair play to them! They're making the best of what they have.'

Bill and Fred seemed not to notice the attention they generated. They made their way around the locality slowly – sometimes *very* slowly, depending on

Snowball's mood – and slowly they became a normal part of life in Knockdown.

⚜   ⚜   ⚜

Katie gave a sigh as she entered school on Friday morning. Miss Reddy seemed in an even more serious mood than usual as she thumbed through the maths and spellings tests. She began to call out the results.

'Tracy Dunne. There's only one "t" in carrot, Tracy. Isn't that right, Shauna?'

'Yes, Miss.'

'What's right?'

'Only one carrot in tea. I mean–'

'You mean you were daydreaming again, Shauna.'

'Yes, Miss.'

'As it happens, your test is next. Sixteen in maths, fifteen in spelling. Room for–'

'Progress, Miss?'

'Thank you, Shauna,' the teacher said drily. 'Autumn has a silent "n", Shauna. Does anyone know of another word with a silent "n"?'

Sarah Sue Walsh's hand went up. Trust old 'Brainbox', Katie thought.

'Yes, Sarah Sue?'

'Please, Miss, "condemn" and "hymn".'

'Brilliant. Good girl, Sarah Sue. Remember those words, girls. Now, Katie Lynch.'

Katie drew in a long breath.

'Fifteen in maths and – oh dear! – twelve in spelling. Not very good, is it, Katie? Not much sign of progress there. "Lightning", Katie. Listen to the word. "Lightning". Try it now.'

'L–i–g–h–t–i–n–g?'

'That's exactly what you have here. "Ning", Katie. Ning, ning, ning! Spell "ning"!'

'N–'

'That's right. If you really try, Katie, you can do it.'

Sarah Sue Walsh's hand went up again.

'Yes, Sarah Sue?'

'She probably thought the "n" was silent, Miss.'

'Very clever, Sarah Sue. She probably did!'

Very funny, Brainbox, Katie thought.

'Ning, ning, ning, ning,' Shauna chanted under her breath.

The morning dragged on. After lunch, Miss Reddy made an announcement.

'Pay attention, children. I have a little project for you, and you have a whole week to work on it: "My favourite place!" Just think about that and collect all the information you can about it. It could be here in Knockdown; it could be where you went on holiday. And if you don't think your favourite place is interesting enough, then you could write about an interesting place anywhere in the whole world. Just find out all about it and make a nice project for me. For next Friday.'

Sarah Sue Walsh's hand went up.

'Please, Miss. Can we use the internet?'

'Of course you can, Sarah Sue.'

'My favourite place is bed,' Shauna whispered. 'What can I write about that?'

Katie stifled a giggle.

'Are you all right, Katie?'

'Yes, Miss. Just trying to think of somewhere special.'

'I look forward to hearing about it, Katie. And don't forget to correct your spellings for Monday. Write each one out three times. We must make progress, mustn't we?'

CHAPTER EIGHT

Katie flopped full-length on her bed. She ran her finger along the snake's spine.

'Come on, Mister Guppy. Think! I've tried and tried and I just can't think of a favourite place for my project. We went to Donegal on holidays last year but it rained most of the time. I used to like Granny's house but now she's in the nursing home and she doesn't remember things properly any more ...'

She twirled Mister Guppy into a coil.

'Actually my *really* favourite place is here with you. But if I did a project on that, they would all laugh at me. Especially Sarah Sue Walsh. I bet Brainbox does her project on Disneyland or Hong Kong or somewhere like Timbuktu. My dad could do a project on Timbuktu. He's always saying to me: "What took you so long? Did you go to Timbuktu for the paper?" or

"You can go to see Snowball on your bicycle. He's not exactly in Timbuktu, you know …'"

'Timbuktu … hmm. I wonder … Miss Reddy did say that it didn't have to be *our* favourite place. What do you think? Really? You're a genius after all!' She tweaked his tail playfully and gave him a big hug.

❖   ❖   ❖

'Big Ted! Big Ted!' Gavin bounced up and down in his car seat as they set off for Walburley Hall.

'I want to see Snowball first,' Katie said.

'Big Ted! Snowball!' their mother sighed. 'You'd think we were going to the circus!'

Katie's heart sank when they discovered Snowball wasn't in his paddock, but when they arrived at the house she saw Bill unharnessing the donkey from the cart in the yard.

'I'm so sorry,' Bill said as she pushed the cart back into the outhouse. 'I had a business appointment in town. Thought I'd be back long before now, but Snowball was in one of his lazy moods. He can be a naughty boy at times. Not to worry. I expect Fred's got the nettle soup ready. She picked a great big bunch of them this morning.'

The nettle soup! Katie had forgotten all about Fred's promised treat. Her mouth began to tingle. She remembered falling into a clump of nettles when she was little and how much it had hurt.

'Go see Big Ted!' Gavin demanded.

'And so you shall, young man.' Bill said with a chuckle. 'I'll tell you what. Why don't you go with your mummy to see Big Ted while Katie and I bring this rascal back to his paddock?'

'Come on, lazybones!' Bill took a firm grip of Snowball's mane and tugged him along. 'He's not a bad old fellow really. I suspect he's not used to pulling two old crackpots like us around.'

'You're not crackpots,' Katie protested.

'Well, some people think so. I actually heard a man in the supermarket call us crackpots; he was so embarrassed to find me standing behind him. I told him not to worry. We've been called worse! I suppose we do look a bit strange, but to us, the donkey and cart is a luxury.'

At that moment Snowball stopped again. Bill heaved and tugged until he decided to move once more.

'A luxury,' she repeated as she fought to get her breath back, 'especially when the donkey behaves himself! Of course, in Africa we had an old jeep.'

Katie opened the paddock gate.

'And when I say old,' Bill continued, 'I mean ancient. It was nearly as old as ourselves! It died several times, but Fred brought it back to life again. She's a wizard with cars and jeeps, you know. She would make up a spare part for the jeep and off we'd go again. Just like Snowball!' She slapped his rump as he entered the paddock.

Katie produced two carrots that she had sneaked from the kitchen at home. Snowball began to munch one of them slowly.

'Hmph! No wonder he's lazy!' Bill said. 'You have him spoiled. He gets no carrots from us!'

Katie ignored her remarks. She had something else on her mind.

'Bill,' she gave the second carrot to Snowball, 'have you ever been to Timbuktu?'

'Goodness me,' Bill laughed. 'What a question! The answer is no, but I've been to Mogadishu! Why ever do you ask?'

'Well, it's like this,' Katie began nervously. 'I have this problem …'

'No, Gavin, Big Ted can't come down on the floor. He has to stay there all the time.' Clare Lynch was growing more exasperated by the moment. She was trying to continue a conversation with Fred, who was busy at the stove in the kitchen, while at the same time keeping an eye on Gavin. Where on earth was Katie?

'I'm sure we'll enjoy the nettle soup, Fred. Well, Katie and I, anyway. Not too sure about Gavin.'

'Up! Up! Up!' Gavin held out his arms to be lifted up. If Big Ted wasn't coming down to him, he was going up to Ted.

'Really, Gavin, you're being a little monster!' She hoisted him aloft. 'What's that, Fred? You've got bananas for Gavin? Did you hear that, Gavin? Miss Fred's got bananas for you — if you're a good boy!'

'Nana for Big Ted!' the little boy cried excitedly.

'He loves bananas,' his mother called out. Gavin squirmed in her arms and tried unsuccessfully to tweak Big Ted's nose.

'Lunch is ready!' Fred called out cheerily, just as Bill and Katie appeared.

'At last!' Clare Lynch sighed. 'I thought you two had gone to Timbuktu!'

Bill and Katie exploded in laughter.

'What did I say?' Clare asked in surprise.

'Private joke, I'm afraid!' Bill said.

'Mum, you're getting to be more like Dad every day,' Katie giggled.

Before they could settle down to lunch, Gavin had to be convinced that Big Ted wasn't hungry. His mother held him high so he could offer the bear one of his bananas, but to her horror Gavin lunged forward and squashed the fruit into Ted's face.

'Gavin! Oh, I'm terribly sorry,' Clare attempted to clean away the mess.

'Not to worry, my dear,' Bill reassured her. 'Now, young man,' she said to Gavin, 'Big Ted had a big, big breakfast this morning, so there's no room in his tummy for lunch. Alright?'

Gavin seemed happy with that explanation and they proceeded to the dining room where Fred began ladling piping hot green soup into the bowls on the table.

Katie shot a worried look at her mother and made a face at the steaming bowl in front of her. Clare Lynch returned a freezing smile to her daughter, a smile that said, *eat it, and not a word – I've had enough hassle for one day*!

Katie sighed, filled her spoon with soup and closed her eyes, hoping for the best, fearing the worst. When she closed her eyes, all she could see were huge tangled clumps of nettles.

She swallowed and waited. It tasted …

'Mmmmm!' her mother cried. 'Delicious! Fred, I'm not leaving here until I get the recipe.'

…quite nice, Katie thought. In fact it's VERY nice!

'Isn't it wonderful, Katie?' Clare gave a hopeful glance at her daughter.

'It's brill!' Katie said enthusiastically.

'Brill?' Fred queried anxiously.

'She means brilliant, smashing!' Clare Lynch explained with relief.

'I hope you like the bread,' Fred said, blushing at all the praise. 'I tried out an Irish recipe.'

'Mmmm. It's lovely!' Clare mumbled through a mouthful of soda bread. 'What a talented cook you are!'

'And Fred's a wizard at fixing cars, too,' Katie added. 'Bill says so.'

Fred shook her head. Her face was beetroot red. 'Bill exaggerates so.'

'Nonsense! You *are* a wizard, Fred. Someday you'll show them!' Bill smiled proudly at her sister.

'More nana!' Gavin shouted.

'Really, Gavin—'

'It's all right,' Fred said. 'We've got lots.'

They chatted about the house.

'Whoever called it "Wobbly Hall" was spot on,' Bill laughed. 'But we're getting there! We're going up on the roof to fix the slates as soon as we find ladders.'

'What! You're going on the roof?' Clare Lynch looked at her in disbelief.

'Of course. Did it all the time in Africa. Not a problem!'

Katie looked across the table at the sisters. They are just amazing, she thought. She felt so proud to know them. And to think some people–

'After all, we're only a pair of old crackpots!' Bill winked at Katie.

'Could I have some more soup?' Katie asked shyly.

'Really, you two!' her mother sighed. 'We'll never be asked here again!'

Fred had already leaped into action and returned from the kitchen with pot and ladle.

'Actually, I might have a teensy bit more myself – if it's in the pot,' Clare Lynch ventured.

'Yes, it is quite "brill" isn't it?' Bill laughed.

❖   ❖   ❖

They waved to Snowball as they drove home.

'So-ball! So-ball! Go see So-ball!' Gavin squealed.

'NO, Gavin! Mummy's in a big hurry – and Gavin has to help her with the shopping,' she added quickly to soften the blow.

Gavin slumped in a sulk in his car seat.

'What a pair, those two!' his mother said. 'They're just–'

'Brill?' Katie said.

'– unbelievable. And talking of pairs, what were you and Bill up to outside? What was so funny about my saying "Timbuktu"?'

'Private joke, Mum. Private joke!'

She looked back as Wobbly Hall disappeared behind the trees.

I just hope the joke works, she thought.

CHAPTER NINE

'Thank you, Sarah Sue,' Miss Reddy said. 'Excellent work. Chicago is indeed a most interesting place and the fact that you visited your Uncle William there last year was a great help.'

'The internet was a great help too,' Sarah Sue added pointedly.

'So was your dad,' Shauna Lacy muttered.

'Indeed! Now, Louise, let's hear about your interesting place.'

Louise Collins began telling about her grandad's farm. Katie gave another anxious look towards the school gate. Miss Reddy was coming nearer to her desk and there was still no sign ... She glanced back at the clock. Almost ten-thirty.

'Isn't that so, Katie?' Miss Reddy snapped.

'Yes, Miss.'

'Do tell us what's so–'

Katie gulped. She was in trouble again.

'Miss! Miss! Look! Look!' a chorus of voices called out from the desks by the window. 'It's the two ladies from Wobbly Hall!'

'Michael and Ralf Schumacher. That's what my daddy calls them!'

There was an explosion of laughs and giggles around the room.

'Girls, please! Manners! Show some respect for the visitors.'

Katie gave a sigh of total relief. Bill and Fred had dismounted from the cart. Fred was tying Snowball's reins to the school gate. The entire class and their teacher watched in puzzlement as the two women strode across the playground to the school door. They heard voices in the corridor. Mr Carey was talking to the women. A few moments later, there was a knock on the classroom door. Mr Carey entered.

'Excuse me, Miss Reddy, but we have two visitors here who say they are Katie Lynch's project. Does that make sense to you?'

'I–I'm not sure,' the teacher stammered, throwing a puzzled look in Katie's direction.

'Maybe Katie can explain?' Mr Carey suggested.

'We have this project on an interesting place,' Katie began, 'and I thought it would be interesting to hear about the part of Africa where they grew up.' She held her breath for a moment, afraid to look at Miss Reddy.

'Wonderful idea!' Mr Carey said. 'Come in, ladies, come in!' He ushered the two women into the room. There were a few titters and whispers from the back of the room, but Miss Reddy quickly froze the offenders into silence with one of her looks.

'I'll tell you what,' the principal announced. 'I'll squeeze my class in here too, if that's all right, Miss Reddy? It will be very educational for them. Better than a school trip, eh?'

Miss Reddy could only smile weakly and nod in agreement. She motioned to Katie to move to the top of the room and everyone else shuffled their chairs closer to make space for Mr Carey's class who stood around the back of the room.

'Perhaps you would introduce your friends to us, Katie?'

Katie was reassured by the smiles of the two ladies as she stood up to introduce them.

'This is Bill and this is Fred–'

More giggles.

'–and they have come to live in Walburley Hall. Their

real names are Wilhelmina and Frederika, but their father always called them Bill and Fred. They used to live in Africa, so I thought that would be a most interesting place, and I've asked them to tell us about it.'

'We think it's a wonderful idea!' Bill announced, 'And we're delighted to do it, on one condition! Tell them, Fred!'

Fred edged forward nervously.

'We'll tell you about Somalia if you'll tell us about Knockdown!'

'That seems a fair deal,' Mr Carey said. 'Go ahead, ladies.'

Bill and Fred bowed in unison to their audience.

'*Nabad,*' they said.

'That's our greeting to you,' Bill explained. '*Nabad* means peace. Now, you can greet us!'

'*Nabad,*' the children chorused.

'And *Nabad gellio* means "Peace go with you",' Fred said, 'so now you know two Somali words.'

'*Nabad gellio*!' the class sang.

Bill moved to where the world map hung on the wall. She pointed to the eastern side of Africa.

'You see where Africa bulges out? That's called the Horn of Africa. That's where we lived. The country is called Somalia.'

'Isn't there lots of famine out there?' Sarah Sue Walsh asked.

'Sadly, yes. And there will be. It's a very dry country. Hot. Dry. Sun all day, every day. Except in the rainy season, which is from March to September. But sometimes there is no rainy season. The crops don't grow. And people starve.'

'We have some photographs!' Fred began rooting in her bag. 'Look! This is me driving our jeep along a dry riverbed.' She held up a second photograph, showing a torrent of raging water. 'That's the same river when the rains came.'

Bill continued her story.

'We lived up here, in the north of Somalia. Our father came there to be in charge of an agricultural college – teaching people how to farm. How to grow maize and to keep camels and goats. There are very few cattle in Somalia. The camel is very important, especially to the nomads, the wandering people. They can pack all their belongings in the *aqul* – a sort of tent fitted on the camel's back.'

'Here's a photograph!' Fred said, holding it up for all to see. 'I took that near Amood, where we lived!'

'Thank you, Fred,' Bill said drily, taking up the chalk and writing CAMOOD on the blackboard.

'Excuse me!' Sarah Sue interrupted. 'Fred called it "Amood", but you wrote "Camood" on the board. Which is right?'

'They both are, I suppose,' Bill replied. 'In Somali, the "c" is silent–'

'Like the "n" in autumn,' Shauna piped up. Miss Reddy flashed one of her looks at Shauna.

'Anyway,' Bill continued, 'as I was saying about the camel. The Somalis eat camel meat and drink camel milk.'

'Yeuch!' came the reaction.

'It's quite nice, really,' Fred assured them.

Bill spotted a basketball in the corner.

'I know what we'll do,' she said, picking up the ball. 'We'll play "Bounce a Question". It's very simple. I'll bounce the ball–'

'Ahem!' Fred interrupted.

'Oh, all right! *We'll* bounce the ball to someone and that person can ask a question about Somalia! Here we go!'

Susan Reilly was first to get the ball.

'Em ... em, what do you have for breakfast in Somalia?' she blurted in desperation.

'That's a silly question!' Sarah Sue Walsh snapped.

'It's all I could think of.'

'No, it's a very good question,' Fred assured her. 'We would probably have sorghum. It's a kind of porridge made from maize. Or some fruit – bananas, melons or mangoes – they grow in the south of the country. And lovely hot tea with lots of cloves and spices in it!'

The questions came relentlessly.

'How did you travel from place to place?'

'Well, we were lucky. We had an old jeep for years,' Bill replied. 'Fred here is a wizard with engines and things. She kept it going forever. I don't know how, because you could never get spare parts. Most people walked. There are no roads, you see. It's all rough terrain …'

'Are there shops like here?'

'The nearest town was five miles away. The "shops" are fairly rough and ready. Sort of market-stalls, really. You could buy meat, clothes, little cakes and sweet things. And matches! Matches are very important …'

'Is there any telly?' Shauna asked, to much laughter from her classmates.

'I'm afraid not,' Fred replied. 'The electricity supply was very weak. You could listen to the radio, though, as long as you had batteries. The Somalis love listening to stories and plays. Travelling groups come around and put on plays. That's great fun. Better than telly!'

'What kind of wild animals do they have?'

'Snakes! Lots of snakes. The Somalis are scared of snakes; they believe snakes can fly! And there's the mongoose. You should see him fighting a snake! He's so quick.'

'I have a photograph!' Fred went rooting again. 'Look! There they are! I took that—'

'Thank you, Fred,' Bill said with a sigh.

Is Bill just a teensy bit jealous of her sister, Katie wondered?

'And there are tortoises. Huge tortoises,' Bill continued.

'Don't forget the birds!' Fred suggested.

'Ever so helpful, Fred. Thank you. Birds of all descriptions. Bee-eaters, owls and weaverbirds. Strange creatures that build their nests upside down—'

'I've got a photograph!' Fred chirped.

Another question. 'What was the scariest thing about living in Somalia?'

'The ju-ju man!' Fred shot out the answer. 'He knew when bad things would happen. He told us—'

'Nonsense, Fred', Bill interrupted, giving her sister a severe look. 'No one believes in that stuff any more. Let's see. Scariest? I suppose the big flood that nearly washed us away, one rainy season.'

'I was more scared of the ju-ju man,' Fred insisted.

And so it went on until at last Mr Carey had to intervene.

'You'll tire these ladies out, children! We have only fifteen minutes to lunch-time and you still have to tell Bill and Fred about your place.'

The visitors' questions took a good half-hour to answer before Mr Carey interrupted again.

'Thank you again, ladies, for a wonderful morning, and thanks to Katie Lynch for thinking of the idea.'

'*Mahad sanid,*' Bill said quietly. 'That means "Thank you" in Somali.'

'And the reply is "*Adan mudan*",' Fred added. 'That means "You're very welcome".'

'All together now, class,' Mr Carey gestured with his hands. '*Mahad sanid.*'

Bill and Fred bowed gracefully as they took their leave.

'*Adan mudan,*' they said.

The children watched in silence as Bill untied Snowball and then waved enthusiastically as their departing guests drove the donkey and cart down the road.

'I don't know how we'll catch up,' Miss Reddy sighed. 'We've lost three class periods: maths, Irish and religion. Perhaps, if we took a short lunch break–'

'Ah, Miss!' the children protested.

'It's not fair,' Sarah Sue Walsh whined. 'They never bounced the ball to me. I had several important questions – not just about breakfast,' she hissed.

Katie watched the two heads bobbing above the hedgerow until they disappeared from view.

'*Nabad gellio*,' she whispered. 'And *Mahad sanid*, Mister Guppy.'

CHAPTER TEN

'Gee-up, Snowball!' Bill clicked. 'We'd like to get home today, if possible!'

Snowball was in no hurry to get anywhere and continued to walk rather than trot, despite Bill's urging.

'I thought we did rather well there,' Bill said and, after a pause, 'although you overdid things somewhat with your photographs.'

'You know what they say: a picture is worth a thousand words!'

'Hmph! There was never much chance of me getting to a thousand words! Oh, come on, Snowball. You're being so ridiculous.' The donkey had stopped in the middle of the road.

'Gee-up. Snowball!' Fred added her voice to her sister's, but the donkey took no notice of her.

'Maybe if you showed him a photograph of Wobbly

Hall he'd get the idea!' Bill said.

Fred ignored her sister's taunt. 'You should have let me talk about the ju-ju man,' she said quietly.

'I didn't let you talk about the ju-ju man, my dear, because they don't *know* about the ju-ju man here. There are no ju-ju men in Ireland.'

'But *we* know about the ju-ju man,' Fred countered, 'and we know what he said!'

'Yes, dear.' Bill deepened her voice and said dramatically: "You will meet my brother in the faraway land and he will make great change in your life!" A lot of silly nonsense! And you are even sillier to believe it.'

'Well, how did he know we were going to "the faraway land" in the first place? We hadn't even decided to come to Ireland at that stage.'

'Oh, use your head, Fred,' Bill said in exasperation. 'What about all those letters from the solicitor in Ireland? That postman was the biggest gossip in the locality. And, let's face it; everyone knew that there was nothing left for us on the farm. So a bit of guesswork and a bit of imagination is all it took.'

'Well, there's nothing imaginary about the ju-ju man. He's real.' Fred said stubbornly, then added with a hint of a smile, 'I have a photograph to prove it!'

'Hmph!' Bill snorted. 'Gee-up, you silly donkey!'

A white van was parked outside the house when the sisters eventually got home. A man stood at the top of a ladder that was propped against the wall over the front door.

'Oh goody!' Bill exclaimed. 'It's the telephone man. At last.'

She leaped from the cart. 'Be a dear, Fred, and turn this naughty boy into the paddock.' She tweaked Snowball's ear. 'And then maybe you'd make some of your delicious nettle soup?' She turned and hurried away to the telephone man before Fred had a chance to speak.

Fred unharnessed Snowball and led him to the paddock. 'You're lucky, Snowball,' she said. 'You don't have a bossy sister. When you don't feel like doing something, then you just don't do it. You're lucky.'

On her way back to the house, Fred noticed that her sister and the telephone man had gone inside. The ladder was still propped up by the door. The nettles could wait. This was her opportunity …

'Mmm! Delicious. You really are a wizard, Fred.'

'Yes, with nettles and motor cars and not much else!'

'Well, I suppose with snooker too,' Bill added grudgingly.

'Oh goody! Does that mean we can have a game?'

'Maybe later.'

I don't really need to get walloped again, Bill thought. 'There's something else I want to talk about. I've had an idea.'

Fred groaned inwardly. She hated when Bill had an idea. It usually meant more work for her.

'You're so wizard with the nettle soup and things—'

'I wish you wouldn't go on about my nettle soup!'

'Shush, Fred! This is important. It's about, well, it's about money, actually. Paying the bills. Keeping a roof over our heads.'

'That's just what I wanted to talk about. I've been up—'

'Oh, really, Fred. Please don't interrupt my idea! You see, you're so good with food that I thought, why don't we set up our own little business!'

'Little business?'

'Yes. Preparing food. Soups, desserts, breads maybe.'

'You mean open a restaurant? Here?'

'No, silly. We would *supply* restaurants. There's a rather posh one just a few miles away – Woodfield House. We could make up a few sample dishes.'

'*We* could ?'

'Well, *you* could. I'd look after the business end of things: orders, delivery, advertising, finance – that sort of thing. You know you're not very good at business stuff. So leave all that to me. You just come up with the food ideas. I've even thought of the name: "Bill and Fred's Pantry"! How's that?' Bill sat back, awaiting her sister's enthusiastic response. It didn't come.

'I'd much prefer "Bill and Fred's Motor Repairs",' Fred mumbled. And why wasn't it "Fred and Bill's Pantry" anyway, she thought to herself, seeing as she would be doing all the cooking?

'Be sensible, Fred. Who's going to come out here to have a car fixed? And you have no tools, no equipment. No, the Pantry is a wonderful idea, even if I say so myself!'

'Where are we going to get the food?' Fred asked. 'We can't just rely on nettles!'

'Correct. What we will do will be very simple things. I've been out through the gardens—'

'The jungle, you mean!'

'Jungle now, but a bit of hard work will restore

them. There are wonderful raspberry canes that just
need some weeding. As soon as the ground is cleared
we can grow vegetables and herbs, that sort of thing. I
can see it now – it will be so wonderful!'

Fred sighed. I can see it too, she thought. Guess
who will be out among the weeds on her hands and
knees. And guess who will be in the house, 'looking
after the business end of things'.

'And you have Mummy's spice-box with all those
amazing African spices that they would never get
around here.'

The spice-box. Their mother's pride and joy. Bill
had wanted to leave it in Africa but Fred would not be
parted from it. Apart from its contents, it held so many
memories for Fred. Cooking with her mother. Special,
warm memories. The spice-box ... Fred was
weakening.

'Well, what do you think?' Bill was still waiting for
her sister's congratulations on her wonderful idea.

'How will we deliver the stuff?' Fred asked. She was
desperately trying to find a way out.

'Really, Fred. You can be so negative at times. Think
positive, dear. We'll find a way. It certainly won't be
with Snowball. Everything would be gone off by the
time he'd get there. We'll find a way. It will just take a

little time. Anyway, we'll have to start on the gardens first. Rome wasn't built in a day, as Father used to say!'

'But you hate gardening!'

'Well, yes, but I'll make an effort, just to get you started.'

'Thanks a lot,' Fred muttered.

'And guess what? I found some garden tools in one of the sheds. So we can get going right away!'

'That's the problem,' Fred argued. 'There's so much to do here. There are stables we haven't even got into yet. And there's the leaking roof.'

'Oh Fred, you really are depressing me. Such an old moaner, you are! You'd worry a hole in a pot. Tell you what! Why don't we play a game of snooker before we start in the garden? That will cheer you up. Just one frame, mind you!'

Fred's face brightened up.

'Best of three?' she pleaded.

'Oh, all right. You're such a bossy boots!'

Fred swallowed hard and said nothing for a few moments.

'By the way, where did you go when the telephone man was here?'

'Go?'

'Yes. You were saying you were up somewhere?'

'Oh. Yes. I was up on the roof.'

'On the roof?'

'When I saw the ladder there, I took the opportunity to have a look.'

'Really, Fred, without anyone holding the base of the ladder? That was quite a dangerous thing to do.' Bill's curiosity got the better of her. 'What did you find?'

'There are a few missing slates. They would be easy to replace. We could take some slates off the sheds.'

'Well, you won't find me going up there. I know we went up on the roof in Africa all the time, but this must be three times the height, and the pitch is very steep. No, we'll have to get a handyman. There's a chap in the village I was told about. I think his name is Moran.'

'Mickey Moran?'

'Yes, do you know him?'

'No. Heard about him, like you.'

Fred had also heard that Mickey Moran was better known as 'Mebbe'. 'I'll be up to you Tuesday, mebbe,' he would say. The 'mebbe' meant that he might, or, more likely, that he mightn't. Well, let him try that on Bossy Bill and see how it worked!

'Anyway. We'll see,' Bill said, rising from the table.

'Now for that infernal frame of snooker.'

'Best of three,' Fred reminded her.

'Yes, yes. I know. But first it's your turn to wash up, Freddie dear!'

❖   ❖   ❖

Katie called to Walburley Hall on her way home from school, but had some difficulty finding the sisters. They were not in the house. She wandered around the yard. No sign of them there. She had seen Snowball in the paddock so they hadn't gone out. Finally she heard voices beyond the stables. She followed the sounds until she located Bill and Fred in the garden. Bill was leaning on a rake while Fred was furiously hacking and slashing her way through waist-high weeds.

'Welcome to Bill and Fred's pantry garden!' Bill announced proudly.

'Hmph!' Fred snorted. 'Watch out for rhinos!'

Bill explained her 'wonderful idea' to Katie.

'Sounds great!' Katie said, 'but you have a lot of work to do!'

'Don't worry,' Bill replied. 'We make a good team and we're used to hard work, aren't we, Fred?'

'Hmph!'

'I just called to thank you for coming to the school. You were brilliant, both of you.'

'We had great fun. Hope your teacher didn't mind!'

'No. Miss Reddy fusses a lot, but she's not too bad. I must tell Mr Carey about your pantry garden. He grows herbs and things. I'm sure he would give you some plants.'

'Oh marvellous,' Bill beamed. 'What a helpful child you are. '

She began rooting in the pocket of her jacket and pulled out a bundle of small slips of paper. She peeled one off and gave it to Katie.

'We're on the phone now. That's our number.'

Bill began to hum a tune to herself and set about raking the weeds that Fred had cut and dug out.

'You see, Fred. We're on our way! I told you!'

'Hmph!' came the familiar response. 'Watch out for the snakes. I just sliced one in two …'

Katie jumped back in fear.

Bill laughed heartily. 'Oh Fred! You have such a wicked sense of humour!' she chortled as she made her way back to the house.

Katie took up the rake and made an effort to help Fred.

'May I ask you something, Fred?'

'Mmm.'

'About the ju-ju man. You seemed very anxious to talk about him at school. What is he?'

Fred began to dig and chop furiously.

'If you don't want to tell me ...' Katie began.

'No. I don't mind. I know you don't have them in Ireland, but we had lots of them in Africa. Sort of a witch doctor, I suppose. Made spells and tried to cure people. Told the future. That kind of thing. He wore a belt of human bones. He used to terrify me as a child. Bill says I'm silly but he did frighten me.'

She stopped digging and leaned on the spade.

'Especially when I found out that he had predicted that our brother would die. And he did. Caught some wretched virus and died. Only six. It finished poor Dad. He never got over it. And the ju-ju man forecast other things – like the big flood. Then, when we were leaving he told us we would go to a faraway land where we would meet his brother–'

'His *brother*?'

'Well, not his actual brother. I suppose he meant another African man. He told us that this man would make a great change in our lives. That's what the ju-ju man said, and I believe him, but Bill thinks I'm just silly. What if he meant a bad change? Like what happened to our brother?'

Fred's face was all screwed up with worry and fear, and Katie tried hard to think of something that would comfort her.

'Well, there are no African men in Knockdown ...' She knew she did not sound convincing.

'Bill keeps telling me that.'

'Does she boss you a lot?' The words escaped from Katie's lips before she realised it.

Fred's face cleared and she gave a little giggle.

'I suppose so. I *know* she means the best. I *know* I worry too much. And I *know* Bill is better at planning things and making decisions. I just wish I wasn't so "wizard" at so many things.'

'Fred!' Bill's voice echoed across the garden.

'Better go,' Fred said with a mischievous smile. 'The boss needs me.'

CHAPTER ELEVEN

'I'll be up to you, for certain sure, Miss Bill,' Mickey Moran said with a tip of his cap. 'In a couple of days. Mebbe Friday. Or Saturday, mebbe.'

'Well, you just make sure you do.' Bill wagged a finger at the wiry little man she had met in the post office. 'Poor Fred is having a hard time in "the jungle", as she calls it. So, Friday, then?'

'Friday,' Mickey agreed. 'Mebbe,' he added as he walked away.

On her way out of the post office, a poster caught Bill's eye. The last line read: 'Details to be announced soon'. A wry smile ran across her face. 'Oh Freddie,' she whispered. 'Oh Freddie, this could be our big chance.'

The persistent drizzle made her anxious to get home quickly, but there was no such urgency about

Snowball. If anything, he went even more slowly than usual. 'Snowball,' Bill cried in frustration, 'you really are a toad. No, you're not – if you were a toad, you would have hopped home by now!'

She was thoroughly wet and miserable by the time she had reached home and unyoked the donkey. She peered into the vegetable garden. No sign of Fred. I expect she's inside making a nice hot lunch, she thought. But there was no sign of Fred in the kitchen either, and there was no response to Bill's calls, which echoed through the house.

'Oh, come on, Fred! This is no time for hide and seek,' Bill muttered. She wandered outside, a little concerned now. She listened. From somewhere she could hear a humming sound, all too recognisable as her sister's tuneless efforts. But where was it coming from? All the stable doors were shut.

'Fred? Fred, where on earth are you?' she called out.

There was a loud creaking noise as one of the great double doors of the 'ivy stable' slowly swung open. They had called it the ivy stable because the doors had become completely overgrown with knotted vines of ivy, so twisted and thick that it had defeated their efforts to get into the stable and reveal its contents.

Up to now, that is. Bill stood open-mouthed as the

ivy parted magically and one door swung open. Fred leaped out into the yard and raised her arms aloft before doing a little jig of delight.

'Fred! Are you all right? What on earth is the matter with you? And how did you manage to open—?'

Before Bill could finish her questions, Fred had danced her way over to her and hugged her sister.

'Fred! Really! Are you ill? What on earth?'

Fred's response was to swing her sister around in a waltz.

'Minx! Minx! Minx! Minx' she crooned.

Bill's concern for her sister's health was quickly changing to annoyance. She grabbed Fred's shoulders firmly and brought the dance to a halt.

'Have you been at the sherry, Fred? We agreed the sherry was only for visitors.'

Fred shook her head and burst into laughter.

'Minx! It's a Minx!' she whooped.

'What's a minx? Will you please tell me what is wrong with you? Fred! Pull yourself together! I really am getting very cross.'

Fred wriggled free of her sister's grasp, took her hand and skipped across the yard to the ivy stable. Bill stumbled behind her.

'I've never seen you like this before, Fred. I really

don't know what to make of you!'

Fred put a finger to her lips as she sidled through the open door with some difficulty. Bill followed. She was startled by fluttering, darting shadows above her head.

'Bats!' Fred whispered.

'Yes, you are, Fred. Totally, totally bats!'

Fred dragged her sister further into the gloom. It took Bill a few moments to become accustomed to the dark. Fred released her hand.

'Surprise!' she squealed in delight.

'What surprise? I can't see anything.' Slowly the light seemed to improve until it revealed the outline before her.

A car! It was a car. Raised up on blocks, covered in dust and bird-droppings, draped in clinging cobwebs, but it was a car.

'My goodness me!' Bill whispered in disbelief. 'But where? How?'

Fred traced her finger over the dust-covered bonnet, ' M–I–N–X, Minx.'

'If I hear that word one more time–' Bill began.

'I'm telling you it's a Minx. A Hillman Minx. Must be nearly fifty years old. Uncle Hubert must have hidden it away all this time. Good old Uncle Hubert!' Fred creaked the driver's door open and peered inside.

'My goodness me!' Bill repeated. She didn't know what else to say.

'I can get it working. I know I can,' Fred insisted. She groped in the half-light for a lever that would release the bonnet. 'Got it!' The bonnet jumped up, sending a shower of dust over Bill.

'For heaven's sake, Fred,' Bill spluttered and coughed. 'Do be careful!'

But Fred was heedless now. She raised the bonnet to its full height, adding to the dusty confusion. Bill staggered to the door, gasping for breath.

A carpet of dust had settled on Fred's hair, but she did not notice it or her sister's absence. She hummed to herself. 'Yes, that's all right – good. Can fix that. New leads needed ... new battery, of course. Oh goody, that's in perfect condition ... hmmm. Lovely, lovely. Minnie-the-Minx ... that's what I'll call you! Bill ... Bill?'

'I'm out here in the rain, trying to get my breath back,' came the reply.

'Isn't it wonderful?' Fred chirped. 'Isn't it the best possible thing that could happen?'

'It *might* be wonderful, if it ever goes again.' Bill sounded doubtful.

'Of course it will go. I'll *make* it go. I know I will.

You're always saying I'm wizard with cars.'

'Oh, all right, Fred. But I'm cold and I'm wet and I'm covered in dust and dirt.'

'You're not jealous that I found it?'

'Jealous? Of course not. Don't be silly. I'm just cold, wet, dirty and hungry.'

'Oh, I see. Is it lunchtime already? You go and clean yourself up. I just want to check a few more things and then I'll make you a nice lunch.'

'Hmph!' Bill grunted.

❖   ❖   ❖

Spinach soup, cheese on toast and banana fritters. Yes, it *was* a nice lunch. Bill was in better form as they sat in the kitchen watching the rain cascade past the window from a leaking gutter overhead.

'How on earth did you get into that stable, anyway?' she asked.

'Well, I was fed up gardening in the rain, so I searched around and found a hatchet. Began hacking away at the ivy. I just had a feeling there was something important in there, and boy, wasn't I right?'

'Yes, but I hope you won't neglect the garden, now that you've found the car.'

'But we need a car. Snowball is impossible.'

'Agreed. But we also need to get our pantry business up and running.'

Fred bit her lip. *We* need … *our* business …

Bill seemed to read her mind.

'I spent ages last night making out brochures about our pantry.' She searched in her cotton bag and produced a brochure. 'Isn't that pretty? Don't you like the colours? I took a lot of care with them. I sent some brochures off in the post today.'

'In the post? But we haven't anything ready yet!'

'Well, we have to plan ahead,' Bill said, adding with a slight air of superiority, 'just leave all the planning and promotional stuff to me. Anyway, we can start with the soups and the homemade breads straight away. And rhubarb puddings, now that you found all that rhubarb in among the weeds. And I had another wonderful idea today – wines! We could make elderberry wine and dandelion wine and use them for flavouring the desserts.'

'You're going to need a car to deliver all those orders – when they come in,' Fred pointed out.

She's right, her sister thought.

'Yes, well, I suppose it's all a matter of balance. Anyway, I also met Mickey Moran in the post office.

I've had quite a successful day, really. He's coming up to help us in a couple of days.'

'Mebbe.' Fred made her best attempt at the local accent.

'I must ask him if he has a ladder. We really will have to get the roof and gutters fixed. I'm sure he has a ladder.'

'Mebbe,' Fred repeated with some glee.

Bill frowned but said nothing and began to clear the dishes away.

Fred looked at the torrent sloshing past the window. 'Well, it's definitely not an afternoon for the garden,' she pretended to sigh. 'I'll be in the garage if you need me.'

She was already scuttling across the yard, out of earshot, when Bill suggested she should check if the saucepans were in position to catch the leaks. There was also the business of that poster she had seen in the post office, but she reckoned her sister had had enough excitement for one day.

Just another thing for me to organise, she thought. Fred is so lucky …

Fred spent the rest of the day in the garage. When it began to get dark, she came back to the house to search for some kind of light that would enable her to spend some more hours working on the car. With some difficulty, Bill persuaded her to stay for a cup of tea and a sandwich.

'I hope you're not going to be obsessed with this car,' Bill said.

'Course not,' Fred mumbled through a mouthful of sandwich. 'It's great fun. I can fix it. I know I can. I'm making a list of parts I need.'

'Not too long a list, I hope.'

'They're mostly small things. Except for a battery.' She noticed the frown on Bill's face. 'But I expect I can get a second-hand one in the village,' she added quickly. 'Now, I need some kind of light.'

'There's an oil-lamp in the library,' Bill said with resignation.

'Oh goody! Thanks, Bill.'

'Don't stay too late. I - I miss you in here.'

But once again Fred was out of earshot.

It was true. Bill really did miss having her sister pottering about near her. Of course, Fred could irritate her, worrying about this and that (and yes, she knew she irritated Fred, too) but she was her sister and she liked her company. They had been companions for a very long time.

❖   ❖   ❖

It was midnight before Fred returned. Bill had gone to bed, but was awakened by a shriek from the hall below. She dashed down the stairs, fearing the worst.

Fred stood at the foot of the stairs, holding the oil-lamp and gaping in terror at the figure before her.

'What on earth's the matter?' Bill called out.

Fred could only point at the glowing green eyes that shone down on her.

'Ju … ju … ju-ju man,' she stammered.

'Oh Fred, really. That's the bear, you silly! It's just the light from your lamp that caught his eyes.'

Fred slumped down on the bottom step. Bill switched on the electric light.

'There! See! It's just the old bear! And you're exhausted. You spent far too long out there.'

'I'm sorry,' Fred sobbed. 'I thought … It scared me so much.'

'Then why don't we get rid of the stupid thing?' Bill snapped.

'No! No! Remember Uncle Hubert's warning,' Fred

pleaded. 'If we moved the bear and something happened, I would never forgive myself. I promise I won't let him frighten me again. I know it was silly.'

Bill felt sorry for her sister, still trembling as she clutched the banister.

'Nonsense! What you need is a good night's sleep and some fresh air. The weather forecast for tomorrow is very good. Ideal gardening weather! Come on, you.' She stretched out her hand to her sister. 'And no more talk of ju-ju men!'

CHAPTER TWELVE

A week later, Mickey Moran arrived at Walburley Hall.

'You promised me you'd be here last week,' Bill said sternly.

'Ah now, I only said "mebbe", Miss Bill. You see, I do have a lot of calls. I had to clean a chimney for Mrs Maguire and then there was a drain blocked at Sullivans'. That was an emergency, you see. I get calls like that all the time—'

'All right. All right. Let's not waste any more time. Fred is out in the kitchen garden, through there.' She gestured towards a narrow passageway.

'Right, Miss Bill. Right.'

'Oh, by the way, do you have such a thing as a decent ladder? We need some work done on the roof.'

'Well, now, I don't have a ladder of my own, but for the window cleaning I do get a loan of one from

Corny Connors. And I'll see him Friday, mebbe …'

'Well, if you see him, maybe you could borrow it next week?'

'Of course, mebbe. I'm an expert at the slates, too!'

'Aren't we lucky?' Bill replied drily, before returning to the house.

✤   ✤   ✤

Fred was on her knees in one corner of the garden. Mickey was impressed at the progress she had made.

'Begor, Miss Fred, you've done a sight of work here. Do you need me at all?'

'Of course I do. There's a whole area there beyond the raspberry canes. That will be for the lettuce. There's a fork over there. You can get started right away.'

'Right so.' He picked up the fork and paused. 'Mebbe I'll have a cup of tea before I start – to settle my nerves, like.'

'Your nerves?'

'Yeah. I'm always nervous starting a new job. Once I have a strong cup of tea, I'll be all right.' He produced a flask of tea from his pocket, struggled to unscrew the lid and poured himself a cup.

'Would you like one yourself, Miss Fred?'

'No, thank you.'

'The tea is a great man for the nerves,' Mickey said, as he relaxed on a pile of weeds.

Fred sighed quietly. A great help we have here, she thought.

Fred stood up to ease her aching back. 'I need a break,' she said. 'Can you keep a secret?' she added in a whisper.

'I'm watertight!' came the reply in an even lower whisper.

She beckoned Mickey to follow her through a tangle of shrubbery to the back of the stables, where a rain-barrel stood beneath a window.

'I hope you're good at climbing!'

Mickey was puzzled. 'Climbing? I'll give it a try, anyway.'

He watched in amazement as Fred climbed onto the barrel and proceeded to worm her way though the window before dropping out of sight inside.

'Come on!' she whispered.

Mickey climbed onto the barrel without much difficulty. But getting up on the windowsill and wriggling backwards through the window almost defeated him. Fred caught his ankle and guided him onto the workbench below. He finally stumbled onto the floor and took some time to get used to the darkened interior.

'God help me, I feel like a burglar! Where are we at all?'

'We're in the garage – and you must keep your voice down!'

Mickey noticed the chink of light through the double doors.

'Pardon me for asking,' he whispered, 'but wouldn't it be a lot simpler to come through the door?'

Fred shook her head. 'Bill would see us. She only allows me in here if it's raining or for an hour on a fine day.'

'Why?'

'Because of this!' She whipped off the blue sheet that covered the car. 'Minnie the Minx!' she said proudly as she ran her fingers along the gleaming bodywork.

'The old Hillman! Well, that beats Banagher!'

'You recognise it?'

'Recognise it? Many's the time I ended up in the ditch because of it. God be with your uncle, but he was a terror on the road with this thing. Neither man nor beast was safe with him. I don't think he could see where he was going, most of the time. The guards eventually put him off the road. Disqualified from driving. We never saw the car again. He had it for donkey's years. So this is where it was!' He scratched his head in disbelief.

'It's going to be back on the road very soon!' Fred announced proudly. 'Bill thinks I spend far too much time on it – I much prefer it to gardening – so I have to sneak in the back way, like we just did.'

'Well, pardon me for asking, but why doesn't Miss Bill do the gardening and leave you to the car?'

Fred gave a curious little laugh.

'Because Bill looks after "the business end of things" and that takes a lot of time and organisation, or so she says. Anyway, I could do with some help here, but we must listen out for my sister.'

'Oh, I'm your man. Mind you, this has all been a bit of a shock to me; a cup of tea might help the nerves first.' He reached into his pocket again for the flask.

Fred sighed in despair. Some help! 'You mustn't say a word to Bill about this.'

Mickey swallowed his tea and turned to reassure her, but Fred was nowhere to be seen. He scratched his head in puzzlement.

'There are two candles on the bench. Maybe you

could light them and hold them for me?' The voice came from underneath the car.

'Mebbe I could.' He lit the candles and held them in place. 'Do you know what I'm going to tell you, Miss Fred?'

'Not really,' came the muffled reply. 'Can you move the candle, please. No, the other way.'

'You're a great little woman to be doing all this.'

'Really?'

'And Corny Connors is just the man for you!'

'I'm sorry to disappoint you – Ouch! – the wrench slipped – but I'm not interested in marriage.'

'Who's talking about marriage? Corny Connors dismantles cars. Old bangers and crashed cars. His place is full of them.'

Fred shot out from underneath the car.

'Tell me more,' she said, 'but please keep your voice down.'

They spoke in whispers for some time. Fred's face glowed in the candlelight as Mickey Moran told her about Corny Connors' junkyard. She must get there, with her shopping list, soon. She would show her sister!

A faint call woke her abruptly from her daydream. She motioned to Mickey to be silent. The call came again, louder this time. It was Bill.

'Quickly! We must get back to the garden! Hurry.' She had clambered up on the bench and wriggled backways out the window before Mickey had begun to move. He had just made it to the window with some difficulty when Fred called back to him.

'The candles! Put out the candles!'

'Ah, blazes!' Mickey muttered as he slithered back onto the floor.

Fred jumped from the barrel and raced through the tangled undergrowth to where she had been working in the vegetable garden. Breathless, she grabbed a spade just as her sister turned the corner.

'Here you are! Why didn't you answer me? What on earth's the matter with you? You look as if you've just run a marathon!'

'Difficult – bit – of – manoeuvring,' Fred panted.

'Manoeuvring? This is a vegetable garden, not a rock garden. Where's your helper, anyway?'

'Oh. He's d–doing his business. He'll be along in a jiffy.'

'Doing his business? What business?'

'Oh, Bill, do you have to be so embarrassing? He's doing his – you know – like we used to do in the bush in Africa.'

At that moment, Mickey Moran staggered through the undergrowth, equally flustered and breathless. It was Bill's turn to be embarrassed now.

'Anyway,' she said, 'I was calling you because I've had some good news. A phone-call from the restaurant at Woodfield House. They want a sample soup and a sample dessert for the weekend. It's a trial only, but if we can really impress them, we'll be on our way! Now, what should we try? That's the question.'

What should 'we' try indeed! Fred thought. I'll never get to Corny Connors with my shopping list at this rate.

'Are you listening at all, Fred? I said we might try your special nettle soup. Or a wild garlic soup? And one of your spiced rhubarb puddings? Oh, this is so exciting, isn't it? Or maybe your banana surprise?'

'Yes, dear.' Fred tried to sound enthusiastic, but her mind was still wandering around Corny Connors' junkyard.

'Well, I'll leave you to think it over,' Bill said, concerned about her sister's distinct lack of enthusiasm. She turned to Mickey Moran. 'And you can get on with doing your business – I mean, your digging.' she added hastily.

Fred resumed her digging. Mickey leaned on a rake.

'She's a bit on the bossy side, your sister,' he said after a while.

'She just likes to be in charge,' Fred replied. 'She's very good, really, with money and things. She's very organised.'

'Still, it seems to me that you do most of the work, if you don't mind me saying so, Miss Fred.'

'Well, at the moment, it certainly seems so,' Fred replied. 'You'd better start using that rake.'

'Right, right. Another little sip to settle the nerves and we'll be flying in no time at all!'

Fred rolled her eyes up in desperation. Well, at least I got some useful information out of him, she thought.

'This Corny Connors,' Fred said casually, 'what are his hours of business?'

'Hours of business?' Mickey laughed. 'Corny wouldn't know what the words mean! He's open all hours, day or night.'

'Even on a Sunday?'

'Even on a Sunday – unless he's out with the greyhounds.'

'Greyhounds?'

'Yeah, he keeps greyhounds. They never win anything, though, but he keeps trying!' He put down his cup. 'Listen, we'd better get to work or that bossy sister of yours will be after us.'

Fred swallowed hard but said nothing.

✤   ✤   ✤

Katie came around that evening to see Snowball.

'Impossible animal!' Bill said. 'Has a mind of his own. Stood in the village street for ten minutes this morning and wouldn't move. I'm sure the whole village was laughing at me. So embarrassing!'

Katie stifled a giggle. Poor old Snowball. He was so unused to work. No wonder he wouldn't move.

'Where's Fred?'

Bill looked at the clock. 'Probably working on Snowball's replacement.'

'Replacement?'

'Don't worry, we're not going to shoot him — though I was tempted this morning. You'll find her down in the ivy stable, working at her dream. You'll see!'

One half of the stable door was fully open. Katie approached cautiously.

'Fred? Are you there?'

'In here,' came the muffled reply.

Katie peered in. The now gleaming car came as a complete surprise.

'Where did you? How did you—?'

Fred startled her by sliding out from underneath the car. She wore grey overalls and her face and hands were smudged with grease and oil.

'It was here all the time! Isn't it wonderful? Minnie the Minx!' she exclaimed, pointing proudly to the name on the bonnet.

'But will it go?'

'Of course it will! Just needs some parts and a good overhaul. Hasn't been on the road for donkey's years, but I'll get it going.'

'I forgot, you're a—'

'Wizard with cars!' Fred completed the sentence for her. 'And a wizard in the kitchen,' she sighed. 'And a wizard in the garden!' Another sigh. 'That's my problem. I'm just too wizard!'

She told Katie about her gardening exploits with Mickey Moran and about the trial order from Woodfield House.

'Of course, it hasn't dawned on Bill yet as to how we get the stuff to Woodfield House. Minnie here won't be ready for that by the weekend.'

Katie thought briefly and said: 'Don't worry! I'm

sure I can persuade Mum to help you!'

'Oh, we couldn't!'

'Yes, you could. I owe you that for helping me with the school project. They're still talking about you. Everyone except Sarah Sue Walsh, that is!'

'Yes, I remember Sarah Sue. I took great pleasure in bouncing the ball over her head each time,' Fred giggled.

'So just leave it to me!' Katie laughed. 'Now, I've got to have a word with a very bold donkey!'

'Snowball's not a bit bold. Bill's just cross because she couldn't boss him!'

CHAPTER THIRTEEN

'Mmm! Looks delicious! Smells delicious!' Miss Purcell, the manageress of Woodfield House Restaurant, was obviously pleased with Fred's soup and the spicy rhubarb pudding. 'I think we'll call this "Miss Fred's Pudding". Has a nice homely sound to it, don't you think?'

Fred gave a little shrug of her shoulders. She was just relieved to have made the delivery on time, thanks to Katie's mother. Bill had been so fussy, hovering in the background, tasting the soup, checking the oven temperature, asking questions. Questions, questions, questions. What's this? How long should we leave it? Did you add the herbs? Is there enough spice in the rhubarb?

'I said, "We'll let you know how things go",' Miss Purcell repeated.

'Oh, s–sorry,' Fred stammered. 'My mind was somewhere else.'

'Well, don't let it wander too far when you're in the kitchen,' Miss Purcell advised. 'Good cooking is all about concentration.'

Fred's mind had been wandering about Corny Connors' scrap-yard, wondering what it might contain.

❖   ❖   ❖

Nothing could have prepared her for the real thing when she called there on Sunday afternoon. She had told Bill that she was going for a walk and was a little surprised that her sister did not ask where she was going, nor did she offer to accompany her. Bill was in one of her strange moods. She was hatching some plan, Fred suspected. A plan that would undoubtedly mean more work for *her*.

Corny Connors' yard was an unbelievable jungle of car bodies: crashed cars, doorless cars, engineless cars, mangled cars stacked crazily on one another. A whole maze of broken, rusting, buckled metal. In and out through the maze wandered an assortment of greyhounds, sniffing, yapping, searching. Fred was relieved to see that they wore muzzles.

Corny's house lay somewhere in the middle of the maze and when Fred finally found her way to the door, accompanied by four curious greyhounds, a very large woman filled the doorway.

'He's down there somewhere.' She gestured towards the lower part of the yard. 'Once he has the dinner, he's gone. Just follow the noise!'

Fred began her search, now trailed by a clutch of noisy hens. Somewhere in the car jungle, a cock was crowing. A deep voice was singing tunelessly and there was the rhythmic sound of metal being hammered. Fred weaved her way though the chaos until she came across a man's rear end wedged in the door of a car.

'Ahem!' she coughed. No reply.

'Excuse me. Mr Connors?'

A startled grunt came from within the car and the man waddled backways out of the door. Fred had to step sideways nimbly to avoid colliding with him.

He turned to face her, a great barrel of a man, bursting out of blue overalls. His red, unshaven moon face showed his surprise.

'Hell's bells! You gave me a start and a half!'

'I'm terribly sorry. I didn't mean–'

'Don't worry about it! You're Miss Frank, aren't you?'

'Miss Fred, actually.'

'Oh aye. "Mebbe" told me you might be over. But you know what he's like: "She'll be over to you one of the days, mebbe," he says. He's a terrible man for the mebbes. Anyway, I hear you found the old Minx!'

'I did indeed. And I was hoping—'

'Hoping I'd have some spares. Well now, it's a long shot but I just might be able to help. What exactly are you looking for?'

Fred withdrew a slip of paper from her pocket. 'I have a little list here.'

He took the list in a great paw of a hand and studied it closely. He scratched the back of his head, grunted, sighed and grunted again before handing back the list.

Fred's heart dropped.

'You can't help?'

'Well, Miss Frank. The truth of the matter is, I never was much good at the reading. Never went much to school. Spent my time hunting and fishing – and looking after these fellows.' He fondled the ears of one of the greyhounds that had gathered around him. 'The wife does all the reading for me.'

'I see,' Fred said quietly. 'Well, this is what I'm looking for.'

She read slowly through the list, now and then

glancing at the moon face for a hopeful sign. A silence followed.

'Hmm. You'd never know, now,' he said at last. 'You'd never know what we might find!' Fred's heart beat a little faster. 'But first I have to get the seat out of this old Ford. I promised it to a fellow up your way last week. So if you have the time to wait ...'

'I've got all day,' Fred said immediately.

The next three hours were the happiest she'd experienced since she came to Ireland. It was heaven to be in this higgledy-piggledy world of broken cars, and talking engines and parts with Corny. Once he had dislodged the seat from the Ford, they wandered through the jungle in search of Fred's list.

Corny would survey a wreck, scratch his head and wonder out loud: 'I dunno. It might work. Mebbe ...'

'You're beginning to sound like Mr Moran,' Fred laughed.

'Oh, that fellow! A right latchico!'

'A latchico?'

'Aye. A bit of a trickster.'

'He's a good help in the garden, though, when he's not drinking tea.'

'That's what I mean, a latchico! He's always—'

'Mr Connors! Mr Connors!' Fred cried excitedly.

'Ah, call me Corny. No one ever calls me Mr Connors.'

'Mr Corny! Mr Corny! Look!' Fred was doing a little jig in her excitement.

'Hell's bells! What's got into you, woman?'

'Your hen-house! Look!'

The "hen-house" was no more than a battered old car that sat in the middle of a fenced-off area. Inside the fence, hens rooted and scratched, clucking contentedly. Some of them hopped in and out of the wreck.

'Well, if it's eggs you're looking for, just ask the missus. That's her department.'

'No, Mr Corny. The car! The car!' Fred was growing more exasperated by the second.

Corny looked puzzled. Then it dawned on him.

'Well, I declare! It's an old Minx, isn't it? Must be there for donkey's years. Sometimes what you're looking for is right under your nose. Hell's bells!'

They marched into the enclosure.

'Shoop! Shoop!' Corny scattered hens to left and right, and brushed straw and droppings out of his way as he wedged his huge frame into the driving seat. 'Stay there now, Miss Frank. This is no place for a lady like you.'

'This is *just* the place for me!' Fred cried. 'Release the bonnet!'

Corny groped under the dashboard and tugged at a handle. Suddenly the bonnet sprang up. Fred raised it higher and peered in. The engine seemed intact.

'Yes!' she whispered. 'Yes! Yes! Yes! It's all here.'

❖ ❖ ❖

The journey home was uncomfortable, but Fred didn't care. She sat in the front of Corny's 'dog-box' – the red van in which he brought his greyhounds to training and races. Normally, there was only a driver's seat in front, but this evening Fred sat in the Ford seat that Corny was delivering to a customer. As the van moved and stopped she slid forwards and backwards on the loose seat. The greyhounds poked their muzzles into her hair but she didn't mind. On her lap sat a large cardboard box full of the parts she needed for Minnie the Minx. It had been a satisfying afternoon but, as the van turned into the driveway for Walburley Hall, Fred's smile turned to a frown. What would Bill say about her absence? About the money …

'There you are, Miss Frank. I'm in a hurry now. You can settle up with me later.'

'Thank you so much, Mr Corny. I really do appreciate your help and kindness.'

'No bother! I'll be looking out for that Minx on the road any day now!'

'I hope so, Mr Corny. I hope so.'

Fred had thought she might sneak down to the garage straight away, but Bill was standing in the kitchen doorway, watching her sister's movements.

'Nice of you to come home again,' she said curtly.

'Sorry,' Fred mumbled. 'I didn't tell you where I was going.'

'I know you didn't, Fred. And that's why I'm annoyed.' She eyed the cardboard box suspiciously. 'Been to a jumble sale, then?'

'Not exactly. A spare parts sort of sale.'

'Spare parts?'

'For the car. Oh Bill, I got everything. We'll have a car in no time now.' Fred's face beamed with enthusiasm.

'Delighted to hear it. I suppose you got all the parts for free?'

'Not exactly.'

'And how much is 'not exactly'?'

'Fifty euro,' Fred whispered.

'*Fifty euro*!' her sister exclaimed in horror. 'Where are

we supposed to get fifty euro?'

'Mr Corny was very nice about it. We don't have to pay him straight away.'

'Which is just as well, since we don't have fifty euro!'

'But it's an investment, Bill. Once we get the car running, we can deliver the food ourselves. Don't you see? Please don't be cross.'

Bill had to admit her sister had a point.

'But it was still irresponsible of you to go off like that. After all, I'm in charge of business matters.'

'I'm sorry, Bill. I was just afraid you might not let me go if I told you.' She looked proudly into the box. 'And this is a real bargain, honestly.'

'Hmph! Maybe so.' Bill was softening, but for a reason. 'Anyway, I've found a way to raise fifty euro – and more, hopefully.'

'You have?'

'Yes. First prize in the snooker competition is five hundred euro!'

CHAPTER FOURTEEN

'The snooker competition?' Fred asked apprehensively, lowering her box to the ground.

'Yes, the snooker competition. Or to give it its full title, The Grand Knockdown Charity Snooker Challenge.'

Fred knew the answer to the next question, but she had to ask it in order to confirm her fears.

'And *who* is going to play in the snooker competition?'

'Don't be silly, Fred! You are, of course.'

'But I can't play–'

'Of course you can. You're always beating me, aren't you?'

'Men! I can't play men!'

'Why not? There's nothing in the rules about excluding women. "Open to all comers," it says. I checked. "'Entrance fee 20 euro. First prize 500 euro'"

'Twenty euro? You paid twenty euro to enter me and you never even asked me?'

'Well, you weren't here, were you? Today was the closing date for entries and I had to take a chance and put your name down. As you would say about the car parts, it's an *investment*, Fred dear, and as the business end of this partnership, I decided to invest in you. You should feel honoured!'

Partnership! Some partnership, Fred thought. *You do the garden, Fred. You make the soups and desserts, Fred. You fix the car – when you have the time, Fred. And now – you play the snooker, Fred.*

'Well, I don't feel honoured,' Fred muttered sullenly. 'I feel terrified.'

'Nonsense, dear,' her sister replied. 'A little nervous perhaps, to start with. But when you get going down in that Community Hall–'

'The Community Hall?' Fred had visions of hundreds watching her every move.

'Of course. When you get going, they'll be the ones to be terrified! Anyway, it will all be over in a week. Win five games and you win five hundred euro. Even if you are beaten in the final, you get two hundred euro.'

'I'm not doing it.' Fred tried to sound defiant, but

the words would only come in a whisper. 'I can't do it!'

'Of course you can, dear.' Bill's voice had become gentle and cajoling. 'Especially when the whole event is in aid of famine relief in Africa. We couldn't *not* support that, could we?'

'Well, just give them the twenty euro, then, as a donation.' Fred was close to tears.

'Come on, Fred. Where's that old Hawkesworth fighting spirit? Looking after Mother? Keeping the farm going? Taking on this place?'

Fred nodded her head slowly. She was crumbling and her sister knew it. Bill put her arm around Fred's trembling shoulders.

'Tell you what. I'll make you a nice cup of tea and we'll have some of your leftover pudding. And then, after you've had a little rest, we'll go down to the library for a game of snooker – just to sharpen you up! Your first game in the competition is tomorrow night.'

❖　　❖　　❖

'Ladies and gentlemen! Order please!'

There was a hush amongst the huge crowd as the master of ceremonies' voice boomed into the microphone. He was resplendent in dress suit and bow tie as he addressed the crowd.

'First round of the Grand Knockdown Charity Snooker Challenge. First match: F Hawkesworth versus C Connors. Play!'

Fred stole a glance at her opponent. It was Corny Connors, but not as she had last seen him. He was slim and athletic-looking in his formal dress: black tailored pants, white starched shirt, bright blue waistcoat and matching bow tie. He grinned at her. An evil, sneering grin. She looked at her own attire. Gardening jumper and jeans. Nobody had told her about dress rules.

All around her, the packed crowd sat in tiered seating. Their faces looked ghostly in the subdued lighting. She looked around for a familiar face. No sign of Bill. Across from her, on the other side of the table, a red light glowed. A television camera! No one had told her there would be television cameras.

The light above the snooker table beat down mercilessly. Sweat rolled off her brow and into her eyes. The cue spun around in her sweaty hands.

'Play!' the man in the dress suit barked impatiently.

Fred played her opening shot. She miscued totally and completely missed the triangle of balls. The crowd sniggered.

'Foul stroke! Connors – four!' the referee announced with a chuckle.

Fred tried again. The heat was intense. Everything became

a blur, but through the mist of sweat, she noticed a chicken flying from Corny Connors' corner and landing with a squawk on the table just as Fred hit the cue ball. It cannoned into the chicken, which fell in a heap on the table. The crowd exploded in mocking laughter.

'Fowl stroke!' the referee guffawed. 'Connors – eight – and one dead chicken!'

The crowd began a slow handclap as the referee removed the chicken and some loose feathers from the table. The cue ball was replaced.

'Last chance, Hawkesworth!' the referee roared. 'No more fowl play, please!'

The crowd laughed and cheered as Fred tried desperately to concentrate. She wiped her brow with the sleeve of her jumper. As she hit the cue ball, she realised, too late, that it was a hen egg. It smashed into a yellow mess and startled Fred so much that she jabbed the cue downwards. It tore into the green baize and ripped it apart for half the length of the table.

The crowd began to throw objects at Fred: programmes, cushions, an ice cream ...

'Off! Off! Off!' they chanted.

'Hawkesworth disqualified!' the referee howled, holding his sides as he laughed uncontrollably.

'No! No! No! Unfair! Unfair!' Fred screamed.

Fred sat upright in bed, confused and shaking. She felt cold and clammy. She looked at the bedside clock. Five past four in the morning. She reached for something to cover her shoulders. Her old gardening jumper was draped over a chair by the bed. As she touched it, the memory of her nightmare returned. She cast it from her and fumbled for her dressing gown. She knew she wouldn't get back to sleep now. There was only one thing to do. She slipped quietly down the stairs to the library, drew back the sheet that covered the snooker table and began to practise.

CHAPTER FIFTEEN

'Fred! Fred! Wake up! It's past ten o'clock! Are you all right? It's not like you to sleep late.'

There was genuine concern in Bill's voice.

'What!' Fred started out of a restless sleep. 'Of course I'm awake – thanks to all that banging!'

Bill peered cautiously around the door.

'I was just worried about you, that's all. You never sleep this late.'

'I only went to sleep at seven,' Fred muttered. No point telling Bill about the three hours at the snooker table.

Bill threw back the curtains.

'Ouch!' Fred cried as the morning sun dazzled her.

'Such a wonderful morning. And we've had wonderful news while you were in dreamland.'

Fred's heart sank. Dreamland! If only Bill knew.

'A phonecall from Miss Purcell!' Bill almost sang the words.

'Miss P–?'

'From Woodfield House. Seems the customers loved your pudding. *And* your soup! So she wants more for tomorrow night. Our first real order! See, I told you, Fred. We're in business! Now that I've let you have a sleep-in, you'll be full of energy. Chop-chop, Fred. There's work to be done.'

Bill was on her way out the door. 'Just as well *I* was up with the lark or we would have missed our first order. Chop-chop, Fred.'

After breakfast, Fred retrieved the box of spare parts from under the stairs. Now that Bill had conceded that they would need the car for deliveries, she didn't have to have an excuse to work on the Minx. But she only made it as far as the kitchen door.

'Oh really, Fred. You're not going down to that dusty old shed on such a beautiful morning?'

'But I have to–'

'You have to get out to the garden and tend to your herbs. We have to build up our stock of ingredients for the soups, you know.'

'But now that I have the parts–'

'And you need fresh air in your lungs after such a

long night's sleep.'

Fred dropped the box on the kitchen floor and sighed.

'That's the spirit, Fred. Anyway, you'll be stuck in that hot snooker hall tonight, so, fresh air, garden, chop-chop! The morning's gone and I'm way behind with my office work.'

Fred bit her lip, grabbed her spade and stomped out to the garden. The first clump of weeds she came upon suffered a violent death. She worked furiously in the garden until Bill called her.

'Lunchtime! I've taken time out from the office to prepare a light lunch for the snooker champion!'

Two small banana sandwiches. A *very* light lunch. It didn't matter. Fred didn't feel hungry.

There was silence in the kitchen. Bill felt uneasy.

'Not eating? You're not nervous about the snooker, are you, Fred? You're such a silly! Once you get started, you'll love it. And you'll win. Look how you walloped me last night.'

'Wasn't hard,' Fred whispered to herself.

'Pardon? I hate when you whisper, Fred.'

Bill reached for Fred's sandwiches.

'Oh well. There's no point in wasting such a tasty lunch. Waste not, want not, as Father used to say.'

Further silence, broken only by the sound of Bill's chewing. Finally she relented.

'All right. I know when I'm beaten! You can have an hour in the garage with that car.' She dabbed her lips with a napkin and gave a loud sigh. 'As if I didn't have enough on my plate, I now have to manage a temperamental snooker star as well!'

Fred didn't hear her sister. She was already halfway to the garage, scuttling along with the box of spares in her arms.

Bill gave another sigh. 'Never even offered to wash up!'

CHAPTER SIXTEEN

Fred talked to herself as she busied herself under the bonnet of Minnie the Minx. Yes! That lead fits perfectly! Now if I can just loosen those nuts. Yes! Oh thank you, Mr Corny, thank you. Corny Connors had given her a special set of spanners he had found in the boot of the hen-house Minx.

Fred was so totally absorbed in her work on the car that she even managed to forget about the snooker competition. And she got quite a start when Katie appeared in the doorway, pushing Gavin in a buggy.

'Oh dearie me! You gave me quite a shock. Never noticed you coming! Hello, little man.'

'More like little nuisance,' Katie sighed. 'He had me pestered to go and visit Snowball. I had to push him all the way over!'

Gavin suddenly became very excited.

'Car! Car! Go in voom-voom!'

'I'm afraid it doesn't quite go – yet,' Fred chuckled. She lifted Gavin from the buggy and sat him behind the steering wheel of the car. Gavin was in his element.

'VOOM! VOOM! VOOM! VOOM! VOOM!'

'We'll never get him out of there now,' Katie laughed. 'Just as well Mum is coming to collect us in a while!'

She watched intently as Fred worked away.

'You won't mind if I don't talk too much,' Fred said. 'The boss has only allowed me an hour.'

'The boss?'

Fred stood up, a screwdriver gripped between her teeth and nodded towards the house.

Katie understood. Big sister.

'But *you* can talk to me,' Fred added.

So, in between Gavin's frenzied bouts of 'driving', Katie told Fred all her news. She had got eighteen in her spelling test and seventeen in maths. Her best ever results. A little sign of progress, Miss Reddy said. Of course Sarah Sue Walsh got twenty in spelling and nineteen in maths ... and she was in tears because she couldn't read Miss Reddy's writing on the blackboard and *that* was why she got one sum wrong. And Miss Reddy said she understood and gave Sarah Sue twenty for maths also. It wasn't fair!

Fred giggled as she listened to Katie's tales from school.

'And I nearly forgot!' Katie continued. 'I must tell you about Dad. He's terrified—'

She was interrupted by the noise of a car clattering across the cobbled yard. Her mother had arrived to collect her children.

Gavin had to be prised with some difficulty out of Fred's car.

'You can go in Mummy's car now,' his mother said as she strapped him into his car seat.

'I think he prefers driving,' Fred said, still working on her engine.

Clare Lynch came over to see what Fred was doing. 'Really, Fred, you're full of surprises! Is there no end to your talents?'

'Bill thinks not, anyway,' Fred muttered.

'And will you really get this car going?'

'Oh yes – a few more days and then we'll go VROOM! VROOM! Won't we, Gavin?'

The boy gave a wail from his car seat.

'Sorry!' Fred said. 'I've started him off again, I'm afraid! But tell me about your husband!'

'My husband?' Clare Lynch was puzzled.

'Yes. Katie was telling me he had some scare or other?'

Clare Lynch turned to her daughter, somewhat bemused. Katie whispered in her mother's ear.

'Oh, *that*!' Clare exploded in a fit of giggles. 'Poor Michael! Just for a laugh I entered him in the charity snooker competition. He really hasn't a clue, but it's for a good cause, and it will be a bit of fun!'

The smile drained from Fred's face.

'That's why he's terrified,' Clare continued. 'He hates losing – at anything. Golf, cards, and snooker, even though he's useless at it. And do you know what has really wound him up?'

Fred shook her head.

'He's been drawn against a complete stranger in the first round. Probably a champion player from Dublin. Someone called F Hawkesworth ...'

CHAPTER SEVENTEEN

'It's *you*!' Clare Lynch was incredulous. 'But we always knew you just as Fred – never thought of your second name.' She paused, then slapped her hands on her knees and fell into uncontrollable laughter. 'Oh Michael, poor Michael. He's so terrified of playing this *champion* from Dublin. I can't wait.'

'Mum! Behave!' Katie was growing more embarrassed with each word from her mother. She had been as amazed as her mother by Fred's astonishing disclosure, but she could see that Fred did not find the situation as humorous as her mother did. Fred was growing very agitated.

'We didn't know you played snooker, Fred. Don't worry! You won't need to be that good to beat Dad, anyway. He hasn't played for years. It was Mum's idea. Just for fun.'

'It was Bill's idea in my case,' Fred replied. 'And not for fun. She expects me to win the top prize.'

Clare Lynch sensed how upset Fred was and now assumed a more serious expression.

'Have you played snooker a lot?' she asked in a genuinely curious voice.

'Well, we played a lot in Africa when we had our own table. I could beat Father then. And then we found a snooker table here in the house. But I only play Bill now. And anybody could beat her!'

'But that's it!' Fred added defiantly. 'I'm not going to play in the competition. Especially against Mr Lynch. I don't know which of us would be the more embarrassed.'

'Oh nonsense, Fred.' Clare Lynch dismissed the objection with a wave of her hand. 'Michael will be fine – as soon as he gets over the shock! And you *must* play! I think it's wonderful to have a woman playing, and an East African champion, too!'

Fred blushed. 'I was never a champion.'

'But *they* don't know that!'

Katie noticed a glint in her mother's eye. A glint of devilment.

'Chop-chop, Fred! Garage time over! Good afternoon, Mrs Lynch, Katie.' Bill was in a no-nonsense mood. 'Fred has an important engagement later on and we must get ready, mustn't we, Fred?'

'Oh, we know,' Clare laughed. 'Match of the century!'

'Oh, we've been talking, have we?' Bill eyed her sister.

'Indeed. Fred is full of surprises,' Clare Lynch nodded. 'And someone else is going to get a big surprise tonight. Ouch!' Clare felt the weight of Katie's foot on her toes. There was an awkward silence.

'Well, we'd better be going,' Clare said. 'I've got to collect Michael – poor Michael!' She slid into the car before the giggles came back.

'Voom! Voom! Voom!' came the chant from the back seat.

'Alright, Mum, what are you up to?' Katie asked as soon as they were well away from the house. 'I saw that look!'

'Oh, nothing,' her mother replied innocently, 'I'm just going to spread a little rumour. Maybe that Fred was East African snooker champion for five years in a row?'

'Mum!' Katie was growing alarmed at her mother's boldness.

'Fun! Just for fun! I want to see their faces! And why

should your poor father be the only one to be terrified?'

'But maybe Fred won't play at all?' Katie pointed out. 'You heard what she said.'

'She must play,' Clare Lynch said firmly. 'For us! For women!'

CHAPTER EIGHTEEN

There were three snooker tables set up in the Community Hall. Play began at seven o'clock. The organisers had decided that, because of the large entry, each game would be restricted to one frame.

Good, Fred thought. I'll be home before they realise who I was.

She slipped in quietly and stayed well away from the tables, waiting for her turn. The crowd was sparse for the early games. Few people gave the woman in the shadows a second glance. Most were intent on the games in progress. There were shouts of encouragement and hoots of laughter at missed shots.

A round of applause as a game ended.

'Game seven. M Brennan versus DJ Daly,' the announcer called.

'Good man, Marty!'

'Go for it, DJ!'

Fred was watching the entrance. The Lynch family had arrived – Michael, Clare and Katie. Fred withdrew further into the shadows. I could leave now, she thought. Tell them I'm feeling unwell. Or just slip out and say nothing. Give him a walkover. Bill would murder me, but I wouldn't care. Bill had not come to the hall. Too busy with 'the business'.

'Game nine. M Lynch versus F Hawkesworth.'

There were a few titters among the crowd.

'F who?' she could hear people say.

Michael Lynch shuffled nervously to the middle table, looking anxiously around for his mystery opponent.

'F Hawkesworth? Is F Hawkesworth here?' the announcer called in his loudest voice.

'Walkover! I demand a walkover!' Michael Lynch joked weakly. 'I knew I'd scare him off!'

'Last call!' the announcer began.

Fred glanced desperately towards the door.

'Fred? There she is! Come on, Fred!' Clare Lynch's voice rang out across the hall. Fred suddenly felt every pair of eyes in the hall staring at her. A hush fell on the hall, broken only by the clack of balls from the other tables and a few whispers.

'Fred?' '*She's* F Hawkesworth!' 'It's her from Wobbly Hall!'

There was no escape now. Fred presented herself at the table. The announcer was totally perplexed.

'Y-you are F Hawkesworth?' he stammered. 'But you are a wom—'

Clare Lynch interrupted him.

'A snooker player! And she's down to play my poor husband. So let them play!'

There was an outburst of laughter.

'I'll-I'll have to consult the organising committee,' the announcer spluttered.

'What's the problem?' Clare Lynch queried. 'Come on. It's only a charity competition. Let's play!'

There was a chorus of agreement. The announcer shrugged his shoulders, set up the balls and, in a voice little more than a whisper, said, 'Play!'

Michael Lynch was more surprised than anyone.

'Is this a joke?' he muttered to his wife.

'No. Just the luck of the draw, dear.'

'Good luck, Dad! Good luck, Fred!' Katie called.

Fred nervously offered her hand to her opponent to wish him well and played the opening shot. By now, the entire attendance had gathered around the centre table.

It was obvious after a few shots that Michael Lynch was by far the weaker player. Fred concentrated on the table. She didn't dare look at the audience, and tried to block out their comments.

Suddenly it was easy. Too easy. Fred's confidence grew and in twenty minutes it was all over. An easy victory for F Hawkesworth. This time Michael Lynch bashfully offered his hand in congratulations.

'Well done!' Clare cried. 'One up for us!'

'Whose side were you on, anyway?' her husband queried.

'Why, on both sides, dear. I couldn't lose!' She turned to Fred. 'Now, we can give the winner a lift home.'

'No, no. It's all right. I can walk–'

'Nonsense. It's no trouble. And I'm sure Bill will be dying to hear your news.'

There was a long silence as the car left the village. Katie felt a little sorry for her father.

'Isn't this the true spirit of sport?' Clare said at last. 'The loser drives the winner home.' She patted her husband's head. 'Poor Michael! Hasn't played snooker for ten years.'

'And won't for another ten!' Michael Lynch muttered. 'I was very rusty.'

'I don't know. You scored some good points.'

'Yeah. Thirteen. Only problem was that Fred here scored eighty!'

'Well, you were up against the East African champion, dear.'

❖   ❖   ❖

'Eighty – thirteen? Well, that was a clear-cut win.' Bill was well pleased. 'Of course, I knew all along you would win easily. Told you that several times. I expect you would like a cup of tea. I've made a fresh pot. I'm off to bed now. Had a busy day. And I suggest you get an early night. Big day tomorrow!'

'Big day?'

'Yes. Remember, we have a restaurant order to fill. And, of course, Round two tomorrow night. Good night, dear – and well done!'

'Good night!' Fred waited until her sister had ascended the stairs before moving into action. She was going to make herself the biggest, yummiest plate of sandwiches ever.

CHAPTER NINETEEN

News of F Hawkesworth and her first-round victory spread quickly around the village.

'You're the talk of the town,' Clare Lynch said, when she arrived to help transport the food to Wood-field House on the following day. 'You'll have a big fan-club tonight!'

'That's what I'm afraid of,' Fred muttered.

'Don't worry. We'll be there as your cheerleaders. Well, Katie and I will. Somehow I don't think Michael will want to go!'

There was a noticeably bigger crowd in the Community Hall that night. Fred could sense a buzz among the crowd when she arrived with Clare and Katie. Her self-appointed cheerleaders were wearing big rosettes with the words: 'We're For Fred!' sewn onto them.

'Mum's idea,' Katie said.

'Brilliant, aren't they?' Clare was very pleased with her handiwork.

'Don't worry,' Katie whispered. 'I spoke with Mister Guppy and he'll do his best for you.'

'Mister Guppy?'

'He's my special friend. He looks after me. I'll tell you later.'

'Game Five,' the announcer called. 'F Hawkesworth vs M Tully.'

Again the crowd melted away from the other two tables and surrounded Fred's table. There were a few shouts of support.

'Good man, Mick! Come on, Tully!'

Fred shook hands with Mick Tully.

'Quiet, please! Play!'

Fred fixed her eyes on the table and tried to shut out the comments from the crowd … She was in Camood. A hot sun filtered through the shutters onto the snooker table. 'I'll beat you this time, Father. Just you wait. I'll beat you …'

Easy. Why was it so easy?

'Game to F Hawkesworth!' the announcer boomed. Loud applause. Clare Lynch hugged Fred.

'You're the greatest!' she shrieked.

Fred shrugged her shoulders. Katie gave her a

thumbs-up sign.

'*Mahad sanid*, Mister Guppy,' Fred whispered to her young friend.

❖   ❖   ❖

Mickey Moran leaned on the garden rake and surveyed his morning's work.

'Well, one thing's for sure, Miss Fred. I never thought I'd be working with a snooker champion!'

'I'm not a champion. I've only won two matches!'

'But aren't you the champion of Africa? That's what I hear them all saying, anyway.'

'Nonsense! They're just silly stories.'

'Mebbe. Anyway, I wish you the best. Especially if you come up against Flash Fagan.'

'Flash?'

'Yeah. Frankie Fagan. "Flash" they call him, because of the way he dresses. Waistcoat, dickey bow, frilly shirt, shiny shoes. Thinks he's one of them television snooker stars. You should see the get-up of him. A right latchico!'

Fred smiled. She remembered Mr Corny using that word to describe someone else … someone who wasn't too far away from her at this very moment!

'It would be great if you could beat him,' Mickey continued. 'Take him down a peg. He's far too big for his shiny shoes.'

'You can rake this patch now,' Fred said quietly.

'Talking of shiny shoes, there was a strange fellow in the village the other day. Shiny shoes, shiny suit, shiny sunglasses. Arrived in this big silver car that was half the length of the street. You never saw the like! A black man.'

'A black man?' Fred dropped her gardening trowel. 'W-what did he want?'

'Don't know. He was making some kind of enquiries. I wasn't talking to him myself. But you should have seen the car. You could live in it!'

Fred was not concerned with the car, but with the man. She remembered the ju-ju man's words: *You will meet my brother in the faraway land and he will change your life.*

Mickey surveyed the sky.

'I think, mebbe, I'll call it a day. There's a spell of rain on the way.'

'Where is he now?'

'Who?'

'The ju–, I mean, the man in the big car.'

'Don't know. Haven't seen him since. Some of the lads were joking that he must be Flash Fagan's manager!'

CHAPTER TWENTY

Mickey Moran's news troubled Fred for the rest of the day. That evening, she was drawn against Darren Power, a young man whose schoolmates cheered his every stroke. Fred found it difficult to concentrate amid the shouting.

'Come on, Darren! Free classes tomorrow if you win! Free classes if you don't win – 'cos you'll be dead, man!'

Clare Lynch was not to be outdone.

'Come on, Fred. Do it for the sisters!'

'Darr–en! Darr–en!' came the chant in response.

'We're for Fred! We're for Fred!' Katie found herself sucked into the excitement.

'Ladies and gentlemen! Please! In fairness to the players. A bit of respect. Please!'

The announcer's pleas eventually quietened the

crowd. Both Fred and Darren played cautiously and matched each other, score for score, until Darren made a mistake and missed a simple shot. Fred took control of the game then and went on to win. But it was nowhere as easy as the first two rounds. She felt sorry for Darren and shook his hand warmly.

'Phew!' She flopped down on a seat by the wall as Clare and Katie came to congratulate her. 'I don't think I will last this much longer,' she sighed.

'Nonsense,' Clare replied. 'You were just being cool. Although I suppose from now on the opposition will be more difficult.'

One of that opposition was about to begin his match. It was Flash Fagan.

'Do you mind if I watch for a while?' Fred asked. 'He might be my next opponent.'

Mickey Moran's description of Flash was spot on. He strutted up to the table, wearing a multicoloured waistcoat and matching dickey-bow, a dazzling white shirt and smart black trousers with a stripe of sequins running down each leg. He carried a polished wood cue-case, which he opened slowly to reveal three cues. He fingered each cue carefully, occasionally glancing at the table, before selecting a particular cue for this match. He made a few practice shots, marching briskly

around the table, whacking the balls with great
authority.

Fred smiled weakly. He might be a show-off, but he
could certainly play snooker. He won his game in fifteen minutes. When it was over, the announcer stood
on a chair and called for silence.

'Ladies and gentlemen, we have made great progress in the Knockdown Grand Charity Snooker Competition. Thank you for your support. Tomorrow will
be a rest day. We resume on Friday with the semi-finals,
for which the draw has been made and is as follows:'

There was complete silence.

'S Sullivan vs E Ryan.'

Oh no, Fred gulped.

'F Hawkesworth vs F Fagan.'

❖   ❖   ❖

'Fred against Flash! Match of the day!' Clare Lynch
chortled as she drove Fred home.

'He's too smart,' Fred sighed. 'I'll never beat him.'

'Of course you will. There's more to snooker than
snappy dressing. Would you listen to me – the expert!'

'What does Mister Guppy think?' Fred whispered
to Katie.

'Mister Guppy thinks if you really want something to happen it will happen. Well, most of the time anyway,' Katie whispered back.

'Tell me about him.'

Katie told Fred about her much-loved snake who had kept giraffes from coming under the door and who now lived in a hatbox in her wardrobe.

'I must meet him sometime,' whispered Fred.

It was such a relief to wake up next morning knowing that she would not have to face the snooker competition that night. She had been woken by a downpour. Fred gave a little chuckle. No snooker. And heavy rain, which meant no gardening either. She could have all day with Minnie the Minx. She skipped down to breakfast, pausing only to move one or two saucepans into position on the stairs.

PLINK! PLINK! PLONK!

What a beautiful, beautiful day, Fred thought.

CHAPTER
TWENTY-ONE

'More good news!' Bill announced over breakfast. 'Woodfield House have been on to me again. They want more stuff.'

'Drat!' Fred muttered.

'Seems they have a big family booking for Saturday lunch. Wedding anniversary. They will need lots of desserts.'

'But I–'

'I'm telling you, Fred dear. "Bill and Fred's Pantry" is going places!'

Fred sighed. There was no point in raising matters like Minnie the Minx, 'Flash' Fagan or 'Mebbe's' half-hearted gardening.

'You'll have to admit it, dear. It was a wizard idea

of mine. Not just the name, but the marketing, the pricing – although I do think when we are a bit more established, we could put our prices up a bit. But you don't need to worry about that, dear. I'll deal with the major problems, as usual.'

Fred bit into her lower lip. Five minutes later she escaped to the garage. At least she could talk openly here.

'Good morning, Minnie!' she sang. 'And how are you this beautiful soggy morning? You and I are going to have a wonderful day together. Who knows? By this very evening I could have your little engine purring and singing to me as we go up and down the roads. Won't that be special? And I promise I will look after you so well that you'll be the envy of every other car in the parish!'

She raised the bonnet and leaned down into the engine.

'So you just let me know where you have any little pain or ache,' she whispered, 'and I'll look after it.'

She worked busily all morning, humming snatches of a tune that she couldn't quite put a name to. This wasn't really work. This was fun. Anytime Bill and her pantry-talk or Flash Fagan came into her head, she hummed even more furiously. She finally realised the tune was 'This Old Man'. Her mother used to sing it to her as she bounced her on her knee.

'... *with a knick-knack paddywhack, give a dog a bone, this old man came rolling home* ... Dance, Frederika, dance!' She would laugh as she rubbed noses with her daughter, her long blond hair tumbling and tickling around Fred's face–

'God bless the work!' A gruff voice startled Fred from her memories. A barrel-shaped figure filled the doorway. Fred rubbed the mist of tears from her eyes.

'Goodness me! It's Mr Corny, isn't it?'

'One and the same. Though there's few if any calls me that!'

'Oh, Mr Corny. If it's the money, I hope–'

'Money?' Corny chuckled. 'What's that? Not at all. There's no hurry. In fact, one of the greyhounds won a race this week, at last! So we're all right for now. I brought you this.'

Only then did Fred notice the heavy article that he held in his hands. It was a car battery.

'Oh goodness me! Oh dear! Oh, thank you so much, Mr Corny.'

Fred was so relieved. She had dreaded reminding Bill that she still had to buy a battery for Minnie.

'Good as new,' Corny said, as he laid the battery on

the workbench. 'So this is the Minx! By dad, we all jumped out of this lassie's way in our day. Your uncle wasn't the safest of drivers!'

'So I gather.' Fred gave a bashful smile.

'She's looking right good and healthy now,' Corny walked around the car, inspecting it with a knowing eye. 'She'll pass the NCT no problem.'

'NCT?'

'National car test. She'll have to be tested before you can tax her. And you'll have to tax and insure her before you can take her out on the road,' Corny pointed out.

Tax. Insurance. The words hit Fred like hammer-blows. More money. A lot more money.

'H—how much do I owe you for the battery?' she stammered.

'Arrah, not a cent, Miss Fred,' Corny laughed. 'But you have to do something for me. That's why I brought it over to you.'

'Do something?'

'Don't worry! From what I hear, it will be no bother to you.' A glint appeared in Corny's eyes. 'All you have to do is beat that Flash fellow tomorrow night. I'm sick of him prancing about the place. And he's always making fun of me and my scrap business — and my greyhounds. Someone needs to teach that latchico a lesson, and you're the one to do it, Miss Fred!'

✤   ✤   ✤

When Corny Connors had gone, Fred tried to banish his words from her mind and recapture her happy mood. But no matter how loudly she sang, it didn't work this time.

I hate it when people expect too much of me, she thought. Mr Corny expects me to beat Flash Fagan. Bill expects me to work wonders in the garden and in the pantry business. I really wish everyone wouldn't expect so much.

She lowered the battery into position and began connecting the leads.

'At least *you* don't expect too much of me,' she whispered to Minnie. 'Although,' she added seriously, 'I expect lots of you!

She worked on through the day. For once, Bill did not disturb her. Fred sneaked into the kitchen when she heard Bill answering the telephone. She quickly made a sandwich and a mug of tea, and escaped to the garage again.

❖   ❖   ❖

The daylight was fading when Fred felt a flutter of excitement run through her body. Maybe this was the moment she had dreamed of? She reached up to a hook on the wall where a pair of keys hung. Please, she prayed. Her heart raced as she inserted a key in the ignition and turned it. A brief rumble from the engine, then silence. She turned the key again. Just a click this time.

Fred shook her head in disappointment as she got out and peered under the bonnet. In the half-light, she tightened the battery leads. She sat in and tried the key again. A sort of cough this time, but a more promising sound. Again. Another, longer cough.

Fred closed her eyes tight, gritted her teeth and made one more try with the key. A cough, a splutter, a couple of shudders that jolted Fred in her seat, and then the engine finally kicked in and stayed running.

Yes! Yes! Yes! Fred gripped the steering wheel tightly and revved the engine loudly until it ran by itself when she took her foot off the pedal.

The music she had dreamed of filled the garage. Not exactly the purring and singing that she had hoped for, but a healthy chugging from an engine that had been silent for fifty years.

Fred kissed the steering wheel.

'Good girl, Minnie!' she whispered. 'I knew you could do it. Chug away, little Minx! With a bit more practice and a little more work from me, you really will be singing!'

She revved the engine for a few more minutes before leaving the car and running excitedly into the house.

'Bill! Bill! You must come—'

'What is that infernal noise, Fred? I couldn't hear myself on the phone.'

'It's Minnie.'

'Minnie who? And please calm down. You're making me nervous.'

'Minnie the Minx. The car. I've got her running! Come on! Fred tugged her sister's sleeve and half-dragged her across the yard. She pointed proudly at Minnie.

A faint smile crossed Bill's face. 'Well done! Well done, Fred. I always said you were wizard with cars. Bit noisy, though. And smoky.'

'Never mind that. She will get better. Now, you must get in!'

'Really, Fred, I don't think so.'

But there was no stopping Fred. She forced her sister into the passenger seat.

'You're not going to *drive* this thing, are you?'

'Of course!' Fred slid proudly into the driving seat.

'Where?'

'Just around – and around – and around!'

For the next five minutes that was exactly what Fred did. She drove around and around and around the stable yard.

'Stop! You must stop, Fred. I'm getting dizzy,' Bill protested.

'I can fix that!' Fred laughed. She stopped, reversed, and drove around and around in the opposite direction.

'That's enough. Stop!' Bill screamed. Fred turned the car into the garage.

'Oh dear, I really feel quite faint,' Bill said shakily. 'You'll have to come in and prepare the tea now.'

Fred sighed. Was that the best her sister could say? Nevertheless, she was only too happy to oblige. She gave Minnie a grateful pat before following her sister into the house.

'I hope you won't get too excited over that car,' Bill said when they were finished. 'You've been grinning like a Cheshire cat all through tea. Remember, there's the garden to attend to, and that big order for Saturday lunch.'

And Flash Fagan tomorrow night, Fred remembered, with a sigh that darkened her grin. She tried to change the subject.

'Who was that on the phone earlier?'

'The phone? Oh, it was just business. Nothing for you to trouble your head about, dear.'

CHAPTER TWENTY-TWO

The first thing Fred thought of as soon as she opened her eyes on Friday morning was the snooker match. She could feel the fear creeping into the pit of her stomach. I must keep myself busy, she thought; must keep my mind occupied. A spell with Minnie would do the trick.

'I'll have to run the engine for a while – just to tune it up,' she announced over breakfast.

Bill looked at her over the rim of her teacup. 'But there's so much to do,' she began. Then, seeing the worried look on Fred's face, she relented. 'Well, for a very short while,' she agreed. 'And then you really must do some gardening.'

'You know I'm playing in this snooker thingy

tonight,' Fred said as she pulled on her boots.

'Yes?'

'It's the semi-final.'

'Only two matches to go! I knew you could do it.'

'But this is Flash Fagan. He's very good. I don't think I can beat him.'

'I don't want to hear that, Fred. Where is that Hawkesworth spirit? Think "I can" and then you will succeed. That's what Father used to say.'

It didn't work very well for him, then, Fred thought, and immediately felt guilty. Poor Father. She shuffled towards the door.

'And, by the way, ' Bill called after her, 'the only reason I haven't been able to attend is that I've been busy with a lot of paperwork. But I will come and see you in the final tomorrow night. That's a promise. Now, it's a lovely day for the garden, so just a little while with that car, remember. Chop-chop!'

If I'm in the final, Fred sighed to herself, which I very much doubt …

❖ ❖ ❖

Minnie was purring better today. Fred would have loved to take her for a long drive, but Bill found lots of excuses to pass by the garage, remarking, 'Time's nearly up, dear' as she did. Eventually, Fred gave in and set about the garden. After an hour of weeding and half-heartedly hacking at a stubborn clump of briars, she laid down her tools. It was no use; her mind just wasn't on it. She headed over to the rhubarb patch and pulled a few handfuls of stalks. Might as well get the desserts ready, she decided. At least Bill couldn't complain about that!

The results of Fred's culinary efforts that afternoon were far from perfect. She did try hard, but she knew that she had often made a better pear and ginger pudding and a better rhubarb spice-pot. And the only surprise about the banana surprise was that Bill didn't go bananas when she tasted it.

'Hmmm! Not your best, but they will have to do. I expect your mind is too much on that car, Fred. It's your cooking skills you need to tune up, dear. '

But it wasn't Minnie that was distracting Fred; it was Flash Fagan.

Clare and Katie Lynch arrived to collect Fred at six thirty.

'Good luck!' Bill called from the doorway. 'I'll be thinking of you. And, remember: think "I can"!'

As the car moved down the lane, Katie tugged and dragged a bundle from under her coat. She kept it hidden from her mother.

'This is Mister Guppy,' she whispered to Fred as she uncoiled the tattered and patched snake. 'Even giraffes are afraid of him, so Flash Fagan hasn't got a chance.'

When Mister Guppy's head finally appeared, it had a huge *We're for Fred!* rosette affixed to it.

'Katie!'

The girl caught a glimpse of her mother's furious face in the driver's mirror. 'You didn't bring that thing with you? Really, Fred, I must apologise–'

'He's Fred's mascot tonight,' Katie announced defiantly.

'He's filthy and tattered and should be in the bin!'

'I don't mind him at all,' Fred said quietly. 'I'll need all the help I can get tonight.'

❖   ❖   ❖

The Community Hall was abuzz with excited chatter. Even though they had arrived early, Clare, Katie and

Fred had to bustle their way through to the one snooker table that now occupied the centre of the hall. Clare and Katie were lucky to find chairs three rows back from the table. Beyond the chairs, the audience stood in a circle five deep. It's like a boxing match, Fred thought. And I'm about to step into the ring with the champion. She twirled her cue nervously in her hands. Her palms were sweating already. Fortunately, she had brought a little towel to dry them. She sat in her chair, awaiting her rival. She fixed her gaze on the table, deliberately avoiding looking at the crowd. On her way through the throng, she had caught a glimpse of Corny Connors' great moon face. He gave her a thumbs-up sign.

Suddenly the hubbub was drowned by a pounding music beat. The crowd parted to make way for Frankie 'Flash' Fagan. He was accompanied by a young man carrying a ghetto blaster, which blared out the triumphal music.

Flash had really dressed up for the occasion. He loosened a black cape from his shoulders to reveal a startling electric blue outfit – matching trousers, waistcoat and dickey-bow. He handed the cape to his assistant, and bowed in all directions. That was the signal for the chanting to begin.

'Flash! Flash! Flash!' roared his fans.

Clare Lynch was not to be outdone.

'We're for Fred! We're for Fred! We're for Fred!' she shouted as she clapped hands. Others took up her chant until the din of the rival supporters echoed around the hall. Katie proudly held Mister Guppy aloft and waved him to the beat.

Flash went through his ritual of opening his polished cue case (Fred noticed that the word 'Flash' had been embossed in silver along the top of the case). He seemed to take an age fingering the cues and glancing at the table before making his selection. From another part of the case he extracted a chalk-block which he used to chalk the tip of his cue.

Although she knew that this was all gamesmanship, Fred felt intimidated. She wiped her hands on the towel again.

The announcer stepped forward with his hands aloft, appealing for quiet.

'Ladies and gentlemen, out of respect for the players, your silence *please*!' The din slowly abated.

'Thank you. This is the semi-final of our Grand Charity Snooker Competition. The best of three frames. F Hawkesworth versus F Fagan. Fagan to begin. Play!'

CHAPTER TWENTY-THREE

Flash Fagan leaned across to shake Fred's hand. His face showed no emotion. Fred gave a little smile as she took his hand. It felt dry and chalky and she was conscious of her own clammy palms.

Shouts of encouragement began as soon as Flash played his first shot. Katie gripped Mister Guppy tightly and whispered in his ear.

'Come on, Mister Guppy. Do it for Fred.'

Fred tried desperately to concentrate and shut out the din. Once again, she tried to imagine herself playing Father at home in Camood, but this time it would not work. The din was too great. The pressure was too much. The cue became greasy. She had to wipe it constantly with the towel. Each time 'Flash' came to the table, he strutted and pranced about, oozing confidence with every shot. The table became a blur to Fred. She felt miserable and played miserably.

'First frame to Fagan,' the announcer called. It seemed they had only been playing for minutes. I want to go home, Fred thought, as she slumped in her chair. But then she would have to face Bill and her lectures about the 'Hawkesworth spirit'.

Clare Lynch looked anxiously at her daughter. 'Would you ever get that mascot to work?' she pleaded.

'I'm doing my best,' Katie replied. 'And so is Fred.'

The second frame began. Flash hitched up the sleeve of his frilled shirt. It revealed a band he wore on his wrist as a sort of charm. Fred gazed intently at the band. It was snakeskin. Snakeskin.

The hall dissolved into a grassy clearing. A young girl stood fascinated, watching a duel begin to unfold. The mongoose versus the snake. The snake coiled and attacked, but the mongoose was always too quick. His beady eye followed the snake's every move until he knew each turn it would take. He fixed his gaze on the snake, waiting, waiting, waiting for the move that would allow him to thrust his powerful head forward and move in for the kill.

'Second frame to Hawkesworth!'

The cheers came in great waves across the hall.

'Fred! Fred! Fred!'

The rival fans roared back defiantly, 'Flash! Flash! Flash!'

'Ladies and gentlemen. Please. Give the players a chance!' The announcer's pleas were falling on increasingly deaf ears.

'Final frame!'

Fred had a focus now – the snakeskin. The mongoose stalked his prey once again. Flash tried to move even more quickly, but she had rattled him and he was beginning to make mistakes. In desperation, he selected another cue and fumbled in his case for a new chalk-block.

The mongoose moved with greater stealth and waited. And waited.

Those seated in their chairs began to stand up.

'Ah, sit down at the front and give us a chance!' those at the back called angrily.

'Ladies and gentlemen. *Please.*' The announcer's voice was drowned out in the general furore. And then the snake made a fateful wrong move. A small mistake, but a crucial one.

'Frame and match to Hawkesworth!'

Clare Lynch gave an almighty whoop, swept Mister

Guppy from her daughter's hands, draped him around her neck and bounded between chairs towards Fred. She threw her arms around Fred's body and hugged her so tightly that Fred could scarcely breathe.

'Oh Fred, you were *magnificent!*' The tears rolled down Clare's cheeks.

Hands reached out to shake Fred's hand. Occasionally she felt a resounding slap on her back. Katie wormed her way through the scrum of bodies until she could reach up and kiss Fred's cheek.

'Ladies and gentlemen! Please resume your seats! We have the second semi-final coming up!' The announcer was growing more and more annoyed at the crowd's lack of attention to him.

Clare shepherded Fred slowly towards the exit. As they reached the door, Fred felt her hand being clasped by two huge paws. It was Corny Connors.

'God bless you, Miss Fred. You surely made our day. I've waited years for this!'

They eventually reached the security of Clare's car. On the way home, Clare sang loudly.

'We are the cham–pions of the world!'

Katie had never seen her mother so excited.

'Mum?'

'... and we'll keep on fighting– yes, what is it, Katie?'

'Could I have Mister Guppy back now? You do look silly with him round your neck.'

'No, you can't! He's our mascot!' she chuckled. She stroked Mister Guppy and burst into song again.

The mongoose smiled to herself.

CHAPTER TWENTY-FOUR

'We'll need a police escort for this woman tomorrow night!' Clare Lynch announced to Bill on their return home. She was still in such an excited state that she didn't notice the quizzical look Bill gave at the strange article draped around Clare's neck.

'You should see the fan club she has!'

'Of course I knew she would make it all the way,' Bill replied. 'If only Fred would have more confidence in herself. If it wasn't for my confidence in her, she would never have entered the snooker competition.'

Fred's mind was elsewhere.

'Can I show Minnie to my friends?' she asked.

'You and that Minnie,' Bill sighed. 'Ah well, I suppose so. I'm off to bed. Had a busy day. And you need an early night too, Fred. Another big day tomorrow.'

Fred was already leading her friends to the garage.

'That's brilliant!' Clare cried as the engine kicked into action.

'Cool!' Katie breathed.

'You're a genius, Fred. So talented!' Clare said in genuine awe.

'I still can't bring her out on the road,' Fred replied. 'I have to have her taxed and insured first.'

'Well, Michael Lynch is the man for you there.'

'Pardon?'

'Insurance. That's his business. We'll drag him up here tomorrow, won't we, Katie?

'That's very kind of you–' Fred began.

'No problem! I just can't get over this. You're a total wizard, Fred!'

'You're beginning to sound like Bill now,' Fred chuckled.

Later, she stole quietly past Bill's room on her way to bed. *Squeak!* Drat! She always forgot that loose floorboard.

'Is that you, Fred?' a sleepy voice called.

'Yes. Sorry, dear.'

As she reached her own room, the voice called again.

'Fred?'

'Yes?'

'Well done. Very well done. Absolutely wizard.'

✤　　✤　　✤

The congratulations continued next morning when Mickey Moran arrived.

'Well, Miss Fred, you certainly took that latchico down a peg or two!'

'Poor Mr Fagan. I hope he wasn't too upset.'

'Upset? Not at all. Best thing that ever happened him. Him and his blue suits. I never saw Corny Connors in such form as last night. You'd think one of his greyhounds had won the World Cup or something! Which reminds me, I have something for you, Miss Fred, from Corny.'

He led Fred around the gable of the house where his bicycle leaned against the wall. Affixed to the bicycle were two long ladders.

'For the roof. For fixing the slates,' Mickey announced. 'I'm not that good at heights myself,' he added as he loosened the ladders, 'so I thought, mebbe, I'd hold the ladder while you go up?'

'I suppose so,' Fred replied, casting her eye up to the

roof to see where she would position the ladder.

'After all,' she sighed as she began her ascent, 'I'm wizard at roof repairs, too.'

The ladder swayed a little as she reached the top and surveyed the roof for missing slates.

'I'd say there's a mighty view from up there,' Mickey called out.

'I didn't come up for the view. You just hold it steady down there.'

She did steal a look behind her, however. A flash of light caught her eye. Halfway down the avenue the sunlight glinted on a car. Not just any car. A limousine. A man got out of the limousine. A black man. With a shiny suit and shiny sunglasses. He held something in his hands. A camera. He was taking photographs of the house. Photographs of Fred.

'Oh no,' Fred gasped in horror. 'The ju-ju man!'

She grabbed blindly at a rung of the ladder and missed. Her body arched back and she lost her balance. She was falling, falling. And then – darkness.

CHAPTER TWENTY-FIVE

'Frederika! Frederika, darling, are you all right?'

The voice was familiar, but distant, echoing. She felt a face pressed against hers. Softness and a familiar scent. Tickling blond hair all about her face. She felt safe and warm.

'I think so, Mama.'

'Oh thank goodness. What were you doing up in that tree, anyway?'

'Weaverbird … I saw a weaverbird's nest.'

'Oh Frederika, you're impossible.'

Long slender arms enfolded her.

'Wilhelmina? Go see if your father is coming.'

'I've only just looked.' Another voice, distant. 'And anyway she's fine. It was only a little fall.'

'Wilhelmina!'

The tickling hair pulled away sharply from Fred's face. Suddenly there was light shining directly over-head. Dazzling light. She turned away from it. A figure in white stood beside her.

'I think she's coming round,' a voice whispered.

'Fred! Fred, dear! It's Bill. Are you all right?' This voice came from the opposite side. The light overhead made everything a blur.

'Mama! Where's Mama?' Fred squeezed the words out.

'Oh don't be silly, Fred. Mama's not here! This is Bill.'

The figure to her left came slowly into focus. It was her sister. But where–?

'You're in hospital, silly billy. Had a nasty fall. Don't you remember? You were on the ladder. You may thank your stars for that laurel hedge. Such an ugly thing – I was hoping to get rid of it – but, thankfully, you landed right in the middle. We had such a job get-ting you out!' Bill gave a little chuckle. 'Your gardener friend wasn't much help. "Mebbe if we did this! Mebbe if we did that!" Fortunately, the Lynches arrived and–'

Another voice broke in.

'If you don't mind, Miss Hawkesworth. The doctor is here now to examine your sister. Perhaps you could wait outside?'

'How is she?' Clare Lynch asked nervously as Bill returned to the waiting room. Katie sat beside her mother, equally anxious to hear the news.

'She's fine, I think. Doctor's with her now. She's conscious again. A bit confused. Asking for her mama, the silly billy!'

'Thank goodness she's conscious,' Clare sighed. 'Poor thing, she must have got a terrible shock!'

'Not half as much as her gardener friend. He swears he was holding the ladder. Dreaming as usual, I'd say. Where's Mr Lynch?'

'Oh, he took Gavin away for a while. He was proving to be a bit of a handful. There's a tea and coffee machine down the hall. Would you like something to drink?'

'Yes please,' Bill said quietly.

They found a table near the vending machine and seated themselves. Bill's brow furrowed as she stirred her tea slowly.

'I do hope she will be all right.'

'Of course she will,' Clare reassured her.

'I know I'm a bit of an old bossyboots at times and I

know you all think I'm very hard on her.'

'No, we—'

'It's just that she needs to be egged on. She hasn't much confidence in herself. Goes back to our brother's death and Father's drinking. He was very hard on her – on both of us – but I was able for him. Fred wasn't. She crumbled. Became very nervous. Worried about everything. Ju-ju men and all that sort of stuff.'

'Ju-ju men?'

'Sort of witch doctor. Makes cures and spells. Tells you what's going to happen. Very common in the area of Africa where we lived. I never believed in him but Fred was terrified of him and believed everything she heard about his powers.' She took a sip of tea and nibbled at a biscuit.

'That's why she needs someone strong to help her. You have to understand. She's my baby sister. I love her. And she *is* wizard at cooking and cars—'

'And snooker!'

'And snooker.' Bill gave a little chuckle, but Clare noticed her moist eyes.

'And you are wizard too, Bill. At planning and organising things.'

'Oh, I don't know,' Bill protested.

'Yes, you are.' Katie spoke for the first time. 'Fred told me so.'

'Did she? Did she really say that?'

Katie nodded. Bill drew a long breath. 'She has to be all right. She *has* to. If anything serious happened to her, I wouldn't know what to do. I really wouldn't.'

The tears had welled up in Bill's eyes by now. Clare moved her chair closer to Bill and put her arm around her.

❖   ❖   ❖

The morning dragged by. They looked through the old magazines that lay scattered around the waiting room. Occasionally, Bill would get up, pace up and down, look out the window, sigh and sit down again.

'Miss Hawkesworth?' The nurse's voice startled them. 'Dr Maguire would like a word.'

Bill stepped nervously into the office.

'Well, Miss Hawkesworth,' the doctor began. There was a long pause as he completed writing a report. 'Good news! Your sister seems to be okay. A few scratches, bruises, sprains, but nothing broken. She's a lucky woman. I gather there's no hope for the laurel bush, though!'

Bill gave a weak smile.

'Just to be sure,' the doctor continued, 'we'll keep her here overnight. Then a few days' rest at home, and she'll be right as rain. No climbing ladders for a while, of course!'

❖   ❖   ❖

'We brought you some daffodils from our garden,' Clare Lynch announced. 'At least, Michael and Gavin did. The crushed heads with no stalks are from Gavin!'

She ruffled her son's hair playfully.

'And Mister Guppy says get well soon!' Katie added.

'You are all very kind,' Fred replied as she fingered a crushed daffodil head. 'I am so sorry for putting you to trouble. I can't really remember what happened.'

'Don't think about it now, dear. You must rest.' Bill she looked out through the hospital window and into the distance. 'Just as well you made those desserts for Woodfield House, eh?' She paused, then went on. 'Pity about the snooker, though. Can't see you playing snooker for a while now.'

'Oh my goodness! I'm supposed to be playing tonight. I'm so sorry.'

'Don't be silly, Fred,' Clare interrupted. 'You've got nothing to be sorry for. We all know you would have won. And anyway,' she shot a look at Bill 'you still have second prize.'

'True,' Bill muttered.

'Now, I think what Fred needs is a bit of peace and quiet,' Clare said, as she scooped the daffodil heads into a bowl, 'so I suggest we take Bill home, deliver Fred's dishes to Woodfield House, tell the snooker people that unfortunately there will be no snooker final, and then tomorrow we'll come back to take Fred home.'

'You are so kind,' Fred replied. 'The snooker people will be upset—'

'Well,' Clare said briskly, 'I know one person who won't be upset. Seanie Sullivan, your opponent, will be a very relieved man!

Gavin tugged at his mother's hand. 'Go see Big Ted,' he demanded.

When they had gone, Fred closed her eyes against the strong light overhead. The tumbling, tickling hair fell all about her face again. She felt warm and comforted.

'Now, Frederika darling, you have a little rest.' The voice was gentle, soothing.

'Papa will be home soon and we'll tell him all about your nasty fall. And meanwhile I'll make you something nice – maybe your favourite cinnamon biscuits.

CHAPTER TWENTY-SIX

True to her promise, Clare Lynch arrived next morning to take Fred home. A very stiff and sore Fred took some time to ease herself into the car.

'No children today?'

'No. Left them with Michael. You would have no comfort with Gavin. He's just impossible. He made a big scene yesterday when we left Bill home. Insisted on seeing Big Ted – your stuffed bear – and then wouldn't leave until he had fed him a banana! I don't know what Bill must think. So no Gavin today, thank you. And Katie is making you a "Get Well" card.'

'She is so kind.'

'The whole village is enquiring about you. All your fans! You're the big hero since you beat Flash Frankie!'

'Poor Mr Fagan! You know, I can remember playing him, and I remember going up the ladder, but I can't remember the accident at all! Something made me fall, but what?'

'Don't worry about it, Fred. Just take it easy and make yourself better.'

'Yes, but there was *something*. I wish I could remember ...'

❖   ❖   ❖

A number of visitors came to see Fred on the following day. Mickey Moran and Corny Connors were first to arrive.

'We came to see how you were, and for the ladders,' Mickey explained, 'but Corny here is going to have a look at the roof first.'

Bill eyed Corny's well-rounded frame.

'Are you sure that's safe?' she asked.

'Of course, Miss Bill. Corny used to work on the buildings, years ago.'

How many years? Bill wondered.

'Well, be very careful. And please hold the ladder steady, Mr Moran. We don't want any more accidents.'

Bill fussed about nervously for the next hour. Every

time she heard a grating or hammering noise over-head, she held her breath, half expecting Corny to come crashing through the ceiling.

Eventually he came down, unharmed.

'I think I got most of them fixed, Mam,' Corny said as he tied the ladders onto the roof of his van. 'If I missed any, just let me know. How is the snooker champion?'

'She's resting. Not quite the champion, I'm afraid.'

'As far as we're concerned she is,' Corny said, rubbing his hands together. 'I never enjoyed anything as much as her beating that Flash latchico! Tell her that for me!'

'Of course. And thank you for the repairs.'

'No problem. We did it for Miss Fred.'

'Indeed,' said Bill.

'And tell her I'll be up to look after the garden tomorrow,' Mickey added. 'Mebbe.'

❖   ❖   ❖

Later in the afternoon there was another knock at the door. Bill peered through the curtain.

'Two cars,' she said to her sister who was resting on a sofa. 'My goodness, you are popular! We'll have to put up a Visiting Hours notice if this carries on.'

It was the snooker organiser, accompanied by Seanie Sullivan.

'We were very sorry to hear of Miss Hawkesworth's accident,' the organiser began. 'We had a meeting of the organising committee, together with Seanie here – he was to play Miss Hawkesworth in the final – and we've all agreed' – he withdrew an envelope from an inside pocket – 'to pool first and second prizes, and share them equally between Seanie and your sister. So here's a cheque for three hundred and fifty euro!'

'My goodness! That's very kind of you indeed!' Bill recovered from the surprise to accept the envelope.

'There's just one thing,' the organiser added. 'The local paper is anxious to do a story about it all, if that's all right with you. There's a reporter and a photographer out in the other car. Just a short interview with your sister and a photo of herself and Seanie holding the cheque?'

'Well, an interview is out of the question, I'm afraid. My sister is still in shock. Of course, he could interview *me* ...'

The reporter took Bill aside while the photographer positioned Fred and Seanie holding either end of the cheque. Fred was uneasy. I hate photographs, she thought. Always get a twitch in my face.

'That's lovely,' the photographer said. 'Hold that now. Nice big smile, Seanie. You're in the money! You too, Miss – you're looking very serious!'

'D–don't like having my photograph taken.' Fred stuttered.

She jumped a little when the flash went off. That light, the camera. It was coming back to her now. The man with the shiny sunglasses. And the shiny suit. Taking photographs. The ju-ju man!

'Bill,' she called weakly. 'Bill, I–I don't feel very well.'

✛   ✛   ✛

'A bit embarrassing, to say the least.' Bill pulled the curtains together and turned to look down at her sister.

Fred drew the covers up to her chin. She felt very cold.

'The photographer got such a fright when you passed out. And I had just started to tell the reporter about "Bill and Fred's Pantry". Think of the publicity we could have got!'

'Bill, it was the ju-ju man,' a tiny voice said from the bed.

'*What* was the ju-ju man? Really, Fred, you're not going to start that nonsense again!'

'But that's what I saw from the ladder. I remember now. The camera reminded me. There was a black man, in a big car, just out there on the avenue. He was taking photographs. And you remember what the ju-ju man said?'

'Fred! I know you've had a fall and you're still in shock. And maybe you did see something that frightened you. But if there *was* a car on the avenue and a man with a camera, then it was probably a tourist. They love taking photos of these old houses. Now, no more of this ju-ju nonsense! You have too vivid an imagination; Mother always said so.'

'But I saw a black—'

'Fred! I don't care if he was pink, blue, yellow or green. I don't want to hear any more about it!'

She strode to the door.

'Now, I have a business to run. There's a bell by your bed. Ring it if you need me'. She paused and gave her sister a stern look. 'But not if it's to tell me about you-know-what!'

CHAPTER TWENTY-SEVEN

Fred gradually regained her strength over the next few days. She spent a lot of time with Minnie the Minx, polishing the bodywork, fine-tuning the engine. Sometimes she just sat in the driver's seat, listening to the purring engine, dreaming of the day she could take Minnie out on the open road.

'There you are!' Katie's voice woke Fred from her daydream.

'Look what we made for you!' She held up a giant 'Get Well' card brightly coloured with drawings of animals and flowers.

'We all did it,' Katie explained. 'Miss Reddy said it could be our art project for the week. Everyone signed it. Of course, Sarah Sue had to show off as usual ...'

Katie pointed to a huge heart shape drawn in the centre of the card. In the heart, Sarah Sue had written:

I heard about your little fall,
Like Humpty Dumpty on the wall
Now I hope you're feeling fine
And that you'll write a poem just like MINE!

'I do feel a bit like Humpty Dumpty,' Fred giggled, 'but at least they were able to put me together again!'

❖　　❖　　❖

By the end of the week Fred was well enough to walk down to the paddock to visit Snowball. She took a carrot from her pocket and offered it to the donkey.

'You mustn't tell Bill,' she warned. 'She would be very cross if she knew I pinched a carrot.'

The donkey munched the carrot lazily.

'And you'll be glad to hear I've got Minnie the Minx going. So you won't have to pull us around in the cart any more. You can just relax and enjoy yourself.'

She was distracted by the sound of a car passing up the avenue. Fred knew the sounds of cars. She could tell that it wasn't Clare's car, nor Mr Corny's van. She peeped through a gap in the hedge just in time to catch a glimpse of a silver car ... a long shiny silver car ...

'half the length of the street,' like Mebbe had said. Her heart began to race.

'Ju-ju!' she panted. 'The ju-ju man has come.' She hobbled along by the hedge as quickly as her sore limbs would allow. Please don't let him hurt Bill! As she struggled across the stable yard, she heard the front door slam.

Too late! What now?

She paused to gulp a few breaths and then crept along the laurel hedge until she was opposite the bay window. She peered through the laurel leaves. There was nothing to be seen at first. Then he came into view. The man she had seen on the avenue. Shiny sunglasses. Shiny suit. He was pacing up and down, waving his arms about. Fred could not see her sister, but the man was obviously talking to her. Maybe Bill was tied up in a chair!

Fred's heart was pounding now. She must do something, quickly. She hobbled back to the garage, started up Minnie the Minx, drove out into the yard and tore off down the avenue without daring to look towards the house. She must get to the village. Get help. Police. Anyone.

'Come on, Minnie!' Fred gripped the steering wheel tightly. 'Don't let me down now.'

She reached the village and could not believe her luck. There was a police car parked outside the post office. Fred braked hard and came to a squealing halt within inches of the squad car.

'Well, well. What have we here?' the sergeant queried.

'You must – the ju-ju – you must ...' Fred blabbered.

The sergeant was looking at Fred's car with great curiosity.

'Is there an antique car show in town?' he asked.

'No, you don't understand. My sister is—'

The young policeman was also examining Fred's car.

'No tax or insurance, sarge.'

'*Listen! My sister is being held prisoner,*' Fred roared. 'You must come at once!'

Sergeant Duffy gave a startled look at his young colleague.

'Now! Before it's too late!'

'All right, ma'am,' the sergeant said quietly. 'Suppose you get in the squad car and take us to where your sister is being held.'

'Thank you,' Fred said. 'I'm awfully sorry for shouting at you, but I'm really worried.'

'No problem, ma'am. You can tell us the story on the way.'

Garda Troy swung the car around on Fred's instructions and headed towards Walburley Hall.

Sergeant Duffy turned to Fred.

'Now, ma'am. If you could tell us the story – in a nutshell?'

'Well, you see,' Fred began excitedly, 'Bill is always telling me I'm imagining things –'

'Hold on! Hold on! Who is Bill?'

'My sister, of course.'

'Oh! Your sister. I thought it might have been the man holding your sister prisoner?'

'No. That's the ju-ju man.'

'The ju-ju man? And your name is?'

'Sorry. My name is Fred. You see–'

'Fred? I see.'

Sergeant Duffy gave a deep sigh. He had a feeling this was going to be a difficult day ...

CHAPTER TWENTY-EIGHT

Sergeant Duffy poked his binoculars carefully through the laurel leaves.

'G-Two, are you in position? Over,' he whispered into the radio beneath his chin.

'In position, G-One,' came the reply.

'I have the suspect in my sight. Large Afro-American male. Sitting opposite his victim. Making a lot of wild gestures with his arms. Pointing here. Pointing there. Don't really know what he's up to.'

'Maybe he's threatening the lady, G-One. Is he armed? Over.'

'Can't establish that. We'll have to take a chance, G-Two. But let's be careful in there. Over.'

'Ready when you are, G-One. Over.'

'Right. Suspect is in sitting room to right of front door. To your left as you enter from the back. We go on a countdown from three. Over.'

Sergeant Duffy crept back to where Fred was sitting in the back of the police car. He could read the anxiety in her face.

'There's no need to worry. We have him now.'

'But supposing he turns violent and takes Bill hostage?'

'It won't arise. Element of surprise. We'll be on top of him before he knows it.' He paused and surveyed the scene once more. 'You're sure that front door isn't locked?'

'To tell the truth, the lock is broken. There's a big bolt, but we never use it. More's the pity. If we had, Bill might not be in danger now.'

'Don't worry about Miss Bill,' Sergeant Duffy reassured her. 'We'll have her out of there before that fellow knows what hit him.' He switched on his radio again. 'Ready, G-Two?'

'All set, G-One. Just say the word. Over.'

'Remember, G-Two. Speed and surprise are our weapons. Stand by. Over.'

He inched his way forward, crouching under cover of the laurel hedge. A final peek at his target. He bent his head towards the radio.

'Right, G-Two. Three, two, one. Go!'

Sergeant Duffy sprinted across the gravel path, took the three steps to the door in one leap and lunged at it with his shoulder.

The door didn't budge. The sergeant rebounded with a shriek of pain and tumbled back down the steps.

Garda Troy had better luck. He charged through the back door, swung left and gave a triumphant cry as he barged into the sitting room. Bill froze in her chair. Her guest shrieked in terror, dashed across to the bay window and tried to hide behind the curtain. His move was to Garda Troy's advantage. He swept past the cowering Bill, picking up a long poker from the fireplace as he did so. He stood between Bill and the terrified man.

'Don't shoot! Don't shoot. Please. I have a wife and family!'

'Calm down now,' Garda Troy said quietly. 'No one's going to shoot you – especially with a poker. Are you all right, Miss Bill?'

Bill could barely manage a whisper. 'Yes, yes, of course I'm all right. Why shouldn't I be all right?'

'Well, you can thank Miss Fred that you're safe and

well. She saw you were in trouble and alerted us.'

The strength came back into Bill's voice. 'Fred! I might have known.'

Garda Troy kept his eye on the man by the window. 'Now, sir, maybe you'd like to explain your presence here? And, while you're doing that, take your head out of the curtain and no sudden moves, please.'

'S—sure thing, officer. No sweat.'

'He's here to make—' Bill began.

'If you don't mind, Miss Bill,' Garda Troy cut in, 'I'd like to hear the story from the man himself.'

Before he could hear that story, Sergeant Duffy shuffled into the room in obvious pain.

'Everything under control, G-Two?' he muttered.

'No problem, sarge. I'm on top of this one. What happened to you?'

'Misinformation, G-Two. A little matter of a bolted door that shouldn't have been.' He gave a cry of pain as he tried to straighten his shoulder.

'Any damage, sarge?'

'I think my shoulder's busted. Now, what have we got here?'

'The suspect is just about to tell us his story.'

The sergeant eyed the trembling man by the window, who now held his hands up in surrender.

'Okay, my friend. Talk! *Aargh!*' He brushed his damaged shoulder against the fireplace. 'It had better be good!'

'I'm Lane Belvedere,' the man began.

'It's your name we want. Not your address,' the sergeant snapped.

'That *is* my name, officer. At least, it's my stage name. I used to be an actor, you see. Mainly television. I was in an episode of 'The A Team' once. Don't know if you folks get that over here. Anyway, I was arrested in the opening minutes, so you might not have noticed—'

'Look, Mr Belvedere. We're not interested in your acting career!' Sergeant Duffy's pain added to his annoyance. 'We just want to know what you're doing here, terrifying this innocent woman.'

'I beg your pardon, sergeant,' Bill interjected fiercely. 'He was not—'

'*Aaaagh!*' Sergeant Duffy absentmindedly raised his injured arm to intervene. 'We'll – hear – your – story – later – Miss Bill,' he gasped. He turned back to the man.

'I'm a locations manager,' Lane Belvedere continued. 'For Scaredycat Television. We make 'The Marbleheads'. It's a big hit in the States. On fifty cable channels. You don't get it over here yet, but you will! It's a real blast – sort of 'Addams Family' meets 'The Simpsons'. Our ratings are way up–'

'Mr Belvedere!' the sergeant interrupted. 'I am in extreme pain. I should probably be in hospital. I am not interested in your ratings. I simply want to know what your business is in this house today. Do I make myself clear?'

'Perfectly, officer. That's the whole point! I'm here to do business with this lady. You see, we're hoping to make 'The Marbleheads' in your lovely, peaceful' – he gave a deep sigh – 'country and I have been looking for a suitable location for the past six months. I eventually found this house and grounds, which would be just perfect. I was in the process of negotiating a deal with this fine lady when you officers came by.'

Sergeant Duffy shook his head in disbelief. 'You're going to make a movie here?'

'No, sir. We are going to make *fifty-two* movies: two series of twenty-six episodes of 'The Marbleheads' in this wonderful house.' He had regained his confidence and was beaming with pride in his discovery.

'Miss Bill, is this true?' Sergeant Duffy asked.

'Of course it's true, sergeant. Mr Belvedere and I were in the middle of delicate negotiations when you lot barged in–'

'We were only acting on instructions.'

'Don't tell me. Fred!'

'Did someone call me?' Fred peered nervously into the room. 'Is Bill all right? Oh thank heavens!' Fred was unaware of her sister's glowering look. 'The ju-ju man–'

'That's enough, Fred! This man is Mr Belvedere and he came here with a proposition that was going to be a big help to us, until your nonsense brought this invasion. You have really dropped us in it this time, Fred. I don't know what he must think of us.'

A mobile phone rang shrilly.

'It's okay. It's cool.' Lane Belvedere reached into an inside pocket for his phone. 'Hello?'

'Yeah. Everything's cool, Miss Mayo.

'Not just yet. We had a little hitch but it's a wrap. Almost.'

'Can I call you back in a little while, Miss Mayo? I'll explain then. Cool.' He switched off the mobile. 'That was Shannon Mayo. The producer's secretary.'

'Shannon Mayo?' The sergeant repeated. 'Why do all you people have names like addresses? And as for marbleheads and ju-ju men, well, I've had enough for one day. Come on, Garda Troy. Drive me to the hospital and leave these people to their – negotiations.' He spat the last word out.

He turned to Fred. 'And as for you, Miss Fred, I have a good mind to charge you with wasting police time!' He saw Fred's face crumple. 'Well, we'll let you off this time. But there is a little matter of tax and insurance for that motor of yours. Don't let me see it on the road again until it's sorted.'

'Yes, sergeant. I'm really sorry, sergeant,' Fred whispered.

Garda Troy turned to Lane Belvedere. 'So you were in 'The A Team'? That's cool. I used to watch that when I was a kid. Did you know Mr T?'

'Garda Troy!' the sergeant bellowed. 'Now!'

CHAPTER TWENTY-NINE

'I have never been so embarrassed in my life.' Bill sounded crosser than Fred had ever heard her. 'I was just on the point of signing a contract with Mr Belvedere for the television series when you and your Keystone Cops burst in on us.' Bill paced anxiously up and down the room. 'I just hope he doesn't change his mind tomorrow.'

'But I was worried about you,' Fred pleaded. 'I thought you were in danger from—'

'Stop! I know what you were going to say and I don't want to hear it. In fact, I want you to promise that you will never, ever mention that creature again. Ever. Is that clear?'

'I suppose so. But he was right. He said we would

meet his brother and that it would change our lives. And we met Mr –'

'Fred!'

Just at that moment the Lynch family burst in through the open door.

'What's wrong? What happened?' Clare Lynch asked breathlessly. 'We saw Fred's car abandoned in the village. And now we see a police car outside. And a big limousine. And a man talking to the Sergeant Duffy.'

'It's all right, Mrs Lynch,' Bill reassured her. 'It was just a little misunderstanding – on Fred's part.'

Fred looked sheepishly at the ground. Bill went on to explain the good news about the television series being filmed in Walburley Hall.

'Cool!' was Katie's response.

'Hollywood comes to Knockdown!' Clare laughed. 'Who would believe it?'

'Maybe I'll get an acting part,' Michael Lynch suggested. 'I used to tread the boards a bit myself.'

'Yeah, Dad,' Katie commented. 'As one of the monsters!'

'Now look here, young lady. I'll have you know–'

The conversation was interrupted by Gavin's loud sobbing.

'Big Ted! Big Ted dead!'

Amid all the confusion, Gavin was the only one to notice that the great stuffed bear had lost his head. His body had toppled over against the mantelpiece.

'Oh my goodness!' Bill cried. 'It must have happened as a result of all the commotion.' She threw a furious look at Fred.

'There's his head!' Katie cried. 'Upside down in the coal bucket.'

Her father retrieved the head. 'Let's see if we can put him together again.'

He stood on a chair and attempted to right the bear's body.

'Ouff, he's heavy,' he exclaimed.' He peered into the headless body. 'Crikey!'

'What is it?' Clare asked anxiously.

'You're not going to believe this!'

He reached into the body of the bear and withdrew a magnificent silver teapot. And then more silverware. Then two ivory tusks. Jewellery. A whole treasure trove that seemed to be never-ending.

The onlookers watched, speechless, as the bear revealed his secret.

'Well, crafty old Uncle Hubert!' Bill sighed at last. 'No wonder we never found anything of value in the house. He hid it all in here! *That's* why he left instructions that the bear was not to be moved from Walburley Hall!'

She surveyed the collection of riches. 'It would certainly have been a tragedy if we had got rid of the bear and had given this lot away!'

Fred looked at the treasure arranged all about her and smiled a little to herself. *She* was the one who wouldn't let the bear be moved. If it had been up to Bill, the animal would have been long gone. But she said nothing.

'Oh my goodness,' Fred suddenly remembered. 'Minnie! I've got to collect Minnie!'

'We'll take you,' Clare said.

'There you are, Gavin!' Michael Lynch fitted the head back on the now upright bear. 'Big Ted all better. Clever Daddy!'

'Very clever Daddy!' his wife said approvingly.

'It has been quite a day,' Bill sighed as the Lynches prepared to leave.

The day wasn't over yet, however. The postman's van ground to a halt outside.

'Well, this is the place for the action, surely,' the postman announced, cheerily. 'I've just met a police car and a limo coming down the avenue.'

'You've seen nothing yet, Tommy,' Clare Lynch assured him.

He handed the mail to Bill.

'Usual selection of bills,' she sighed.

'At least you'll have the money to pay them now.' Michael said.

'Oh no!'

'What's wrong now?' Fred asked.

'It's a letter from Milly,' Bill replied as she scanned the letter in disbelief.

'Who's Milly?' Clare enquired.

'Cousin. Distant cousin,' Fred explained.

'Not half distant enough,' Bill added ruefully. 'Proper nuisance. Came to visit us in Africa for a week. Stayed for a year.'

She read from the letter: 'Can't believe my luck. There I was, reading the local paper and whose picture do I see but my two lovely cousins. And all the time, here I am, only thirty miles away in this awful retirement home. I said to myself I must pay them a visit straight away – so I'm coming this weekend.'

'Oh dear,' Fred sighed. 'Oh dearie me!'

'Not to worry,' Clare said, trying to reassure the sisters. 'She'll probably stay just for the weekend. Or a week at most.'

'Oh no,' Bill replied with a huge sigh, 'not Milly! Short for Milton Shakespeare. He's an actor. Or rather, he was an actor a long time ago. His real name is Archibald Woolnut.'

Bill gave a nervous laugh. 'And just wait until he hears about "The Marbleheads"!'

CHAPTER THIRTY

Minnie the Minx purred to a halt in the driveway of Katie's home. Katie and her mum raced out to meet Fred, who was bouncing out of the driving seat.

'Well, how did it go?' Clare asked. She already knew the answer from the beaming smile on Fred's face.

Fred gave a little jump and rubbed her hands. 'Passed! Minnie passed her NCT. No problem!'

'That's brilliant!' Clare shrieked, giving Fred a warm hug.

'It's Minnie that deserves the hug,' Fred replied, a little embarrassed.

'Nonsense. To get a fifty-year-old car through the National Car Test. That's just—'

'Wizard?' Fred suggested.

'Indeed! Wizard!'

'Well done, Fred – and Minnie,' Katie added. She gazed in admiration at this amazing little woman who stood by her car, running her fingers affectionately along the roof.

'Well, come on in,' Clare said. 'We must celebrate this great occasion!'

'Afraid not,' Fred sighed. 'Bill needs an urgent delivery to Woodfield House. So it's "chop-chop, Fred"!'

'We'll celebrate later, then,' Clare announced.

'Don't go just yet,' Katie blurted as she turned to dash into the house.

Clare and Fred exchanged puzzled glances. Katie soon re-emerged with Mister Guppy curled in her arms.

'He was your snooker mascot,' she said quietly. 'He should be your car mascot now.'

'But he's yours,' Fred protested.

'He's ours. And I want you to have him.'

Katie climbed into the back seat and draped Mister Guppy along the rear window. He was a perfect fit.

'There, Mister Guppy,' Katie whispered. 'No giraffes will get in here! You'll have much more fun here than in my wardrobe.'

'Well, if you insist–' Fred began.

'I insist. And so does Mister Guppy!'

'Well, thank you, Katie. *Mahad sanid*,' she added with a wink.

'*Adan mudan*,' Katie whispered in reply.

'And there's more good news,' Fred chirped. 'The producer has found a role for Snowball in "The Marbleheads"! He's going to be a television star!'

Mother and daughter waved goodbye to Fred as she swung Minnie out onto the road.

'That was a really nice thing to do, Katie.' Clare put a reassuring arm about her daughter.

Katie shrugged her shoulders as she watched the car disappear, a familiar figure bobbing up and down in the rear window.

'He just seems happier there,' she said.

And she felt happier too.